WonderRama

B.L. Blocher

The Emerald City Press—Southington, CT
ISBN: 978-1-7374610-2-9
Library of Congress Control Number: 2022906189
Title: *WonderRama*
Author: B.L. Blocher
Digital distribution | 2022
Paperback | 2022

This is a work of fiction. The characters, names, incidents, places, and dialogue are products of the author's imagination, and are not to be construed as real.

Introduction

I t's a scary world out there, especially with the likes of these socio and psychopathic deviants running amuck in the shadows of our communities. The blessed fact is that many of these individuals typically end up in prison because of their irresponsible behavior and disregarding of the rights of others, and their inability to distinguish between right and wrong. Oddly there is no clinical difference between a sociopath or a psychopath, other than the later tends more to be criminally violent. But neither are actually an official clinical diagnosis. The true clinical term is : Antisocial personality disorder or ASPD. Individuals with ASPD tend to be men, however I have known a few women who I suspected to be psychopaths (Just sayin'). Some of these individuals may have extreme anti-social attitudes. They are manipulators, and have no conscience, remorse or empathy. And, oh yeah, they are typically pathological liars. Unfortunately, there are no drug treatments for this type of mental disorder, only sessions of psychotherapy, which will hopefully bring light to their antisocial behavior, with the hopes of them possibly changing their ways. ASPD may not be the worst disorder in the world to have, unless it happens to be compounded with other mental issues such as schizophrenia or multiple personality disorders. Then it could be a serious problem.

It can manifest into delusional, violent and perverted behavior. Compounded with all the other red flags of psychopathy, it's a recipe for disaster. I'm not claiming

to be a legitimate authority on the subject matter, but I've watched enough Crime TV to recognise the tell-tale signs of those perpetrators, and they always end up hurting or killing people, in a very disturbing way. I've never entertained the idea of writing a psycho thriller. The problem with writing this type of story is, you have to think like one of these mentally disturbed deviants. You have to literally get into the fox hole with one of these psychopaths and burrow into their thoughts. And, once I started thinking like one, could that in turn bring out the fact that even I have psychopathic and schizophrenic thoughts and ideas??? It sounds like the making of another book. An author who writes about the mentally deranged, who in fact is one of them himself! No, that sounds too unbelievable, even for one of my stories. And so this story goes....

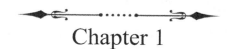

Chapter 1

Security was tight and on high alert at the Denver courthouse.

Armed policemen with military style assault rifles were stationed all around the perimeter of the courthouse building as the SWAT team was positioned on building rooftops overlooking all access points of the building.

The high security was not to protect the witnesses or the court employees from an assault, but rather to protect the community from a particular psychopath who was on trial, if he were to possibly escape from the courthouse.

It was an irregular occurrence when one of the nation's most criminally insane and psychotic maniacs was due to appear in court on a "petition of release" judgment hearing, which he had recently filed with the district court.

His name was Oscar Demento. A deranged psychopath who possessed the ability of superhuman strength whenever he became distraught or agitated.

It was eight years ago, December 25,1995 on Christmas day and at the tender young age of 10, when he bludgeoned his entire family to death with a metal baseball bat, and then decapitated them all with a butcher's cleaver.

His dearly departed family consisted of his two parents and two older teenage stepsisters, Claire and Monica.

Later that same day, the police discovered him oddly trotting along like an ape in the nearby park.

He was covered with blood splatter and dragging a large soggly Santa's sack behind him, just as he was entering the park's basketball courts.

When the police confronted him and asked him why was he all bloody and what was he dragging around in the sack?

He just laughed and replied;

"These are my Christmas presents from my family, "Basketballs" and I'm Satan Claws, ho, ho, ho!" and then he casually reached into the sack and grabbed hold of his stepsister Clair's tangled and blood drenched hair, and pulled out her hideously hacked off head, and shot it up towards the basketball hoop.

The officers at first thought it was some sort of Halloween gag basketball, but then realized that the gruesome head was too realistic, and did not bounce at all once it hit the pavement, but rather landed and cracked like a watermelon.

Oscar was immediately apprehended and sent to a juvenile detention prison.

However, he had to be kept in an isolated and restricted area due to the heinous nature of his crime and his severe demented psychopathic tendencies, to protect the other inmates.

The court hearing was very disturbing, and he was assigned a court appointed attorney, a young woman named Marie Larosa.

She was straight out of law school and believed that even the worst of the worst criminals were entitled to representation.

That was until she met Oscar, and she found it extremely difficult to deal with him, let alone represent him in court.

All he did was maniacally stare and cuss at her as he was securely shackled to his courtroom chair, and referred to her as a "Slut" just like his mother and stepsisters.

The evidence was stacked against Oscar, and he was constantly causing a ruckus in the courtroom.

Everyone was relieved when it was the final day of his hearing.

He was escorted from the detention center by an army of guards and brought into the courtroom, his legs and wrists were once again shackled to his chair.

That's when he immediately notified his attorney that he needed to go to the restroom, just as the hearing was about to begin.

"Hey Slut, I need to take a shit!" Oscar crudely stated.

"Why didn't you go before you came to court?!" she brashly replied.

He faceously stared at her and stated;

"Because YOU wouldn't let me go, and now I'm gonna shit in my pants!" Oscar exclaimed.

"You never asked me about going to the restroom, Oscar! I never even saw you until 20 seconds ago," she retorted.

"Yes I did, you whore! Now you better get me to the bathroom before I shit in my pants or it's gonna

be on you for depriving my bodily needs!" Oscar smugly stated.

His attorney became frustrated and she stared at him, waiting for him to burst out laughing and admit that he was just joking.

"Ehhh, never mind, I'll just take a dump in my pants right here, right now, and empty the courtroom!" Oscar jeered, and then he coyly grinned as he began to clench his face and strain to push.

His attorney was panic stricken as she rushed over to a young US Marshal named Dwain Djokovitch, and reported the situation to him.

The Marshal calmly walked over to the young boy, and without any hesitation he took hold and dragged the chair which Oscar was shackled to right out through a restricted side door and into a caged room similar to a prison cell, which contained a toilet and sink.

It was a holding cell next to the courtroom where criminals were contained and kept during recesses and bathroom breaks.

He was accompanied by another US Marshal and they both began removing little Oscars shackles, releasing him from his constraints.

When Oscar was finally free, Marshal Djokovitch pointed to the toilet and ordered him to;

"Go"

Oscar then smugly took a short step toward the toilet and then turned back towards the US Marshals who were watching him intently, and it was obvious that they weren't happy about having to stand there and wait for him to relieve himself.

"A little privacy please, or are you guys into watching kids pulling their down pants, too?" Oscar sarcastically stated.

The Marshals became uncomfortable at his remark, since neither of them wanted an accusation surfacing that they were inappropriate with a young boy, and so they turned their backs on him, just as he began unzipping and dropping his pants.

As their backs were turned, Oscar seized the opportunity and lunged for Djokovitch's gun holster, and pulled his revolver!

The Marshal quickly turned back, realizing his side arm was compromised!

Oscar laughed and with his child sized hand, pointed the revolver at the other Marshal and instantly pulled the trigger, shooting him in the left side of his chest!

Marshal Djokevich desperately lunged and jumped on Oscar before he could get another shot off, and he tried to take hold of the gun, jambing his fingers between the hammer and the breech as he covered the pistol with his hand!

Both of the Marshals were under attack as Oscar went into a full blown psychopathic rampage.

Despite Oscar's young age, and only being ten years old at the time, his supernatural condition intensified his strength, and he was extremely aggressive and strong!

The Marshals did everything they could to protect themselves from Oscar's outrageous assault.

Once they heard the gunshot and furious shouting which followed, a multitude of guards came rushing into the room!

However, only Marshal Djokevitch had the key to the cell, and he and the other wounded Marshal were locked inside the cage, and fighting for their lives!

The Marshals were quickly losing ground when finally the wounded Marshal was able to get a choke hold on young Oscar, and only then Djokevitch was able to twist the gun away from him, and he quickly stumbled over and unlocked the cell door.

The anxious guards all came charging in and piled on top of Oscar, and they were finally able to restrain him.

After that ordeal, the Judge deliberated for about 5 minutes before returning with his verdict.

Ultimately, Oscar was ordered to be confined at the Colorado mental health facility in Pueblo, an ultra high security asylum for the criminally insane, for an indefinite period of time.

He was kept there in a private secure room, tucked away in a restricted area of the asylum.

Because of his volatile and dangerous nature, he was never allowed outside and never had any visitors.

Basically, there was no one who wanted to see him anyways, other than a handful of tabloid magazine reporters who were always turned away.

It was later revealed by his Aunt Sue, that it was her husband, his Uncle Ned, who had deliberately left the wrapped baseball bat for Oscar as a gift, hidden far under the Christmas tree, as so it wouldn't be found until Christmas day.

When Oscar discovered it under the tree, his parents were mortified that his uncle had actually given him an object that he could use as a weapon against them.

Oscar's father delicately tried to take the bat away from him, begging Oscar to hand the bat over to him.

But at that instant, Oscar realized that he was in possession of something dangerous, which his father feared.

He immediately began obliterating ornaments hanging on the Christmas tree with powerful swings of the metal bat, and he shouted, "Home run!" after each glass ornament burst into tiny shattered glass fragments.

That's when his father frantically grabbed at the bat, and then all hell broke loose!

Oscar yanked the bat away from him and then unconscionably began unleashing his vicious assault against all of his family members. Beginning with his father, the strongest one.

He viciously clubbed him several times across the head, cracking his skull wide open.

Next in line was his screaming and horrified mother as she tried to run away and escape from the house.

He grabbed her by her bright red hair, yanking her head back toward him as he swung the bat with his other hand and repeatedly bashed in her frontal lobe!

Then all that was left were his two teenage stepsisters who were still upstairs and asleep.

He climbed up the stairs in an awkward monkey gait and crept into his stepsister Claire's frilly lavender bedroom.

He crouched down and snuck up to her bed, and then he bashed her skull in with several decisive swings as she slept!

tree, where they joined their parents who were curled up on the floor in pools of blood, next to the lavishly decorated Christmas tree.

He dashed out to the garage, still impersonating his awkward monkey trot and retrieved his massive butcher's cleaver, which he had hidden in there behind a utility cabinet.

When he returned, he joyfully sang Christmas carols as he began to methodically decapitate them all, and then he stuffed their gruesome heads into a Santa's sack which was a Christmas decoration that was hanging from their fireplace mantel.

Indirectly, the police felt it was his Uncle Ned's fault that his brother and his entire family were so heinously murdered, knowing Oscar was a ticking time bomb.

But it was not against the law to give a 10 year old boy a baseball bat for Christmas, and so he was never charged for incitement.

Unbeknown to the police, Uncle Ned was jealous of his brother's wealth and fortune, and Ned constantly looked for ways to cause his brother grief, and to get retribution for his own dire and squandered financial situation. And now he might just benefit financially from his brother's death.

Oscar had been locked up in the mental institution for over a year, and when he was just eleven and a half, he was given certain privileges and allowed to have a special teaching tutor to school him.

Legally, he was required to get some form of an education, even though no one ever suspected he would be getting out of there any time soon, if ever.

Her name was Tracy Fernandez, and until she could get a permanent job teaching in the public schools, she had to settle for working in the prisons and mental institutions in the area.

Oscar was actually progressing and behaving himself, and Tracy was taking a liking to him.

She always requested that his hand shackles be removed while she was teaching him, so that he could write freely with his crayon.

Although as an eminent precautionary measure, there were always several orderies always present in the room with them.

She couldn't understand how such a soft spoken and gentle soul such as Oscar, could have done such a horrific atrocity.

And she mistakenly began to trust him.

Tracy came to see Oscar every week, and they both looked forward to their sessions, and she would reward Oscar for doing his schoolwork, sometimes with candy or baseball player trading cards.

After a short period of time, Oscar had confessed to her that he didn't want to hurt her feelings, however he disliked baseball cards, and seeing the baseball bats some of the players were holding on the cards, reminded him of what he had done to his family.

He requested that if it was alright with her, despite it being off season, he would prefer vintage basketball cards.

And so the following week, rather than baseball cards, she revealed to Oscar that she had brought him an unopened pack of vintage basketball trading cards

that she had discovered in a sports memorabilia store, and purchased them for him as a gift.

Oscar was thrilled, considering that no one ever showed him any form of kindness in the asylum.

He carefully picked up the plastic film wrapped pack of sacred cards and opened it.

Then he delicately removed the long rectangular, rock hard, stale stick of gum that was always included with sports trading cards, and with some effort, diagonally snapped it in two.

The smaller piece he tossed in his mouth, and he held onto the other longer piece in his hand, for later.

He then smiled and then began rifling through the cards as Tracy happily watched on.

"Look! I got a Larry Bird card!" Oscar exclaimed, and Tracy enthusiastically leaned over the table to see it.

Then suddenly without any reason or cause, Oscar's demeanor quickly changed and he lunged at her!

He quickly took hold of her long black hair wrapping it around his fist and pulled her head back exposing her slender throat, and with the hard jagged stick of gum pressed between his fingers, he repeatedly stabbed and slashed her throat!

The orderlies threw themselves on him and he fought them furiously.

It took six orderlies to finally subdue him, and it wasn't until they were able to inject him with multiple syringes filled with a cocktail of strong opiate sedatives.

Badly beaten and injured, the orderlies quickly tried to wrap Tracy's lacerated throat, but she had bled out before an ambulance could arrive.

When the psycho-therapists asked Oscar why he did it, since Tracy Fernadez was the only person who had shown him any form of kindness and compassion? He responded;

"She was a slut, and had it coming."

Following that incident, he was then placed in a padded cell and was locked in there for weeks at a time.

Several months later, there was another court hearing regarding the Tracy Fernandes's murder, and so because of Oscar's young age, the judge had no other options and ordered that Oscar should just continue to remain in the hospital indefinitely.

What else could they do with him?

He was still an adolescent juvenile and a totally deranged psychopathic killer.

During his time at the asylum, the doctors discovered that Oscar's extreme condition of intermittent explosive personality disorder and supernatural strength was due to two irregularities in his brain.

His Amygdala, and Hypothalamus were massively enlarged and he had abnormally enormous adrenal glands in his body.

His fight or flight stimulus response mechanism was exacerbated due to the overwhelming amount of adrenalin which was massively produced and triggered by his enlarged hypothalamus when he became agitated or had anxiety.

These were the contributing factors to his rage and violent aggression.

His inability to control his temper and sexual craving made him into the psychopathic deviate that he was.

When he was in a situation of conflict or anxiety, his hypothalamus would flood and stimulate his adrenal glands to produce massive amounts of adrenaline.

In Oscar's case, 300 times more than the normal human quantity.

And to make matters worse, it was instantaneous.

In less than a fraction of a second, he could be transformed into a powerful super psychotic killing machine.

There were no medications or treatments that he benefited from, but they quickly discovered that once he was enraged, it was nearly impossible to stop him.

With one exception, the drug Metoprolol.

This anti-adrenal blocker drug acts on the effects of, and blocks the over stimulating actions of adrenaline.

The only problem with it was that it had to be injected into Oscar, which meant you had to get close enough to inject it into him, which would be nearly impossible in Oscar's case.

Their only other option was to surgically remove or laser the enlarged organs in his brain.

However, since the laws had changed regarding performing psychiatric operations without the consent of the patient, and there was no way Oscar would ever approve or agree to that.

It seemed that from the onset of his life, Oscar was a problematic child.

He was always upset and angry as a baby.

He could never be soothed and his terrible two's turned into his family's horrific two's.

His parents did somewhat manage to control him when he was small, and when they were finally able to enroll him into kindergarten, they thought that they would at least have some peace while he was in school.

But it didn't last very long, and Oscar was immediately expelled after his first day of kindergarten.

He had badly beaten his kindergarten teacher when she caught him molesting a disabled classmate behind the coatroom door.

His teacher shook him harshly and threw him against the wooden storage cubbies where he hit his head.

As she turned her back and was attending to the little girl, Oscar noticed his head was bleeding and he became enraged!

He quickly took notice of a metal fire extinguisher hanging from a hook, and he aggressively took hold of it, and began furiously beating it against his teacher's head!

The children in the classroom were frightened and they all rushed out of the classroom screaming in distress, as they emptied into the hallway.

When his teacher finally collapsed onto the floor unconscious, he continued on with his rampage and began ripping off her clothes and tearing at her limp body with his fingernails!

Finally the school's principal came rushing in to investigate the tumult, and with the help of two other teachers they were able to restrain Oscar.

No charges were brought up, but he was expelled indefinitely.

His parents were distraught and didn't know what else to do with him.

No private school would accept him no matter how much his father was willing to pay, and so they tried to fruitlessly school him at home.

He basically controlled the house, and all they could do was to try to keep him calm and lock him up in his room at night, so at least they could sleep without the fear that Oscar might escape from the house or attack them in the middle of the night.

At one point they believed he was possessed by a demon and so they called in a priest to attempt an exorcism.

But whatever was holding on to his demented soul, it was too powerful.

The priest was so battered and beaten by the boy that he left the church and became a homeless vagrant living under a bridge on the outskirts of town.

Nothing at all worked to change Oscar, and so they just tried to shower him with love, and hoped for the best.

The daily adage in the household was; "Please.... don't piss off Oscar!"

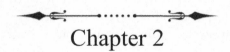

Chapter 2

Prior to this present day court hearing, Oscar had been locked up for over 8 years in the psychiatric hospital where upon recently turning eighteen, he was then transferred to the ADMAX (Administrative Maximum security prison) for adults, located in Florence, Colorado.

The mental institution was just not equipped to control or confine such a violent and psychotically insane killer such as Oscar, even though he was still just a teenager.

And so it was decided by the chief psychiatrist and the hospital's board members to transfer him to the ADMAX prison where he could be better controlled and managed.

Inconceivably, not long after arriving there, Oscar petitioned the court for his immediate release from the prison, stating that his State and Constitutional rights had been violated, and that since the state laws mandated that "no" juvenile offender shall be held for any crime beyond the age of 18, that he should legally be released from the prison.

His complaint was accompanied by the following argument;

"The defendant's claim is; Being that he was technically "Released" by the supervising doctors from the mental facility, Oscar Demento argues that in his own defense, that "Released" must be

interpreted that he was of sound mind and body to be released from the mental institution, and therefore if the doctors believed otherwise, they should have never released him from the mental institution in the first place."

The psychiatric team from the hospital put up a strong fight to keep him imprisoned, stating that he was an extreme threat to society and he would certainly, without a doubt, kill again.

And that he was not actually "released" from the psychiatric asylum, but rather transferred to a more suitable institution to hold him.

They also revealed to the court his personal records and his countless sadistic, masochistic and perverted acts while he was incarcerated at the mental institution.

However, Oscar argued that the ADMAX was not a mental facility and the psychiatrists knew that he would not receive any form of psychotherapeutic treatment there, and so they must have actually believed that he did not need any further mental health care, and the past records they presented were extremely exaggerated and falsified.

"No one could possibly be that deranged. Besides, even if there was a shred of truth, it was all prior to my eighteenth birthday and I've been rehabilitated, thanks to my good doctors."

The trial carried on for several days.

Oscar had been dressed in an oversized thrift store suit and wearing shackles, compliments of the Sheriff's department.

The stakes were high for Oscar, and he was on his best behavior.

When he took the stand, he stated that he was a victim of child abuse, and his family was physically and sexually abusive towards him, but the treatment he recieved from the hospital was effective and cured him, and he was not the same person.

The prosecuting attorney was struggling, and the judge didn't have very many options other than to mandate Oscar to take a cognitive psychological competency examination, to prove that he was no longer a threat to society.

An expert psycho-therapist admitted the PCL-R (Psychotherapy Checklist-Revised) test to Oscar, which was commonly given to inmates and the criminally insane alike.

The test is used to determine whether an individual is psychopathic and devoid of human emotion.

If they are cold, remorseless and impulsive.

Or, if they are bound by nature to be violent and to do harm to others.

Incredibly, Oscar managed to outsmart the system, and was given a clean bill of mental health!

He scored in the lowest range of clinical constructs of psychopathy, and he wasn't surprised considering it was part of his diabolical plan;

"Whatever the question was that the psycho-therapist asked him, he would choose or reply the exact opposite answer of what he actually felt or believed his answer should be."

When he was questioned about his childhood, he said he was a happy child and loved celebrating events with his family.

Despite the truth being that he hated his family, and he had to be locked in his room during most

festivities for everyone's safety (Christmas was the exception).

When Oscar was questioned about his family's pets, he replied that he always wanted a dog.

However, because of his sister's severe allergies to animals, they were never allowed to have pets in their house.

But he confessed that he loved all sorts of animals and aspired to become a veterinarian some day.

Truth be told, he had a dreaded fear of cats and when his father surprised him with a puppy for his 6th birthday, hoping that a pet would help solve his mental issues, it was tragic.

Inconceivably, Oscar tortured and killed that poor puppy just days later by pouring caustic drain cleaner down its throat, "just to see what would happen".

There were scores of other sadistic instances whether it would have been a cat, dog or any other unfortunate animal for that matter, that by bad luck had wandered into his yard.

Oscar would subtly bribe the poor creature closer with some food and a kind voice.

Then bash the unsuspecting animal over the head with either a metal spade shovel or the back of his butcher's cleaver!

He would then proceed to disembowel the dazed animal with his hunting knife, and then carefully carve out it's beating heart!

Then fondle it as he felt it beat and continue to pulse in the palm of his hand, and then he would viciously squish it with his bloody fingers, squeezing the remaining blood out of it, and then paint it on his face as if he were an Indian warrior.

There were other times when Oscar would just simply catch the animal and tie the poor creature up to a tree and pour gasoline all over it, then light them on fire and cut them loose.

Oscar was a true stone cold psychopath, who had no regard or compassion for the lives of animals or people.

However, he was inconceivably able to pass the PCL-R test, and he beat the system.

In reality, rather than receiving the highest score of psychopathic mental disorder, had Oscar given truthful responses, he actually received the opposite...the lowest score on the PCL-R test.

Proving that he was sane and far from the off the charts deranged psychopath that everyone suspected he was.

And so, despite his previous records of outrageous acts of aggression, the law was on his side and the whole country was awaiting to hear the judge's verdict.

Should Oscar be freed or sent back to prison?

That was the question the entire country was waiting to hear the Judge answer too.

The courthouse parking lot was filled with national and local television broadcast trucks and their crews.

The reporters were jammed into the courthouse hallways, hoping to catch a glimpse of Oscar and the decision.

Suddenly there was a loud announcement from the court clerk, who shouted out, and it echoed throughout the hallway that the judge was preparing to return to the court, and he was prepared to render his decision.

Oscar was returned to the courtroom, hobbled and wearing a straight jacket, his legs shackled and wearing his orange striped prison uniform.

It didn't matter anymore how he was presented to the judge, considering the verdict was in.

It was expected that the judge would do the right thing and rule in favor of the State, overruling Oscar's objection and to continue on with his incarceration at the ADMAX prison.

Considering the brutality and heinousness of the acts that he had portrayed, the ruling seemed to be obvious.

The gruesome slaughter of his entire family, the cold and remorsless murder of his teacher, and his violent explosive behavior.

It was apparent that he would immediately be returned to the ADMAX Florence facility for the rest of his life.

There was immediate and grave concern however, that once the judge delivered his verdict, Oscar could react in an explosive and aggressive manner, and become violent in the courtroom.

Even though Oscar was shackled and restrained in a straight jacket, he was so powerful that there was always cause for concern.

As Oscar impatiently sat there in his restraints, he couldn't help but notice the young and beautiful court stenographer sitting across the room, as she prepared her stenotype machine.

Her name was Rebecca Kannon.

She had recently graduated from a local community college and landed the job as the court stenographer.

She was only 23 years old and after living with her parents all her life, she decided to finally move in with her 26 year old boyfriend of the past two and a half years.

His name was Charlie Rama and he worked as a pharmacist in a local drug store.

Rebecca's parents, being devout southern Baptist Christians and her father was actually their church minister, were firmly against them living together, but she was over 18 and they couldn't stop her from being with the love of her life.

To appease them, Charlie stated that they would soon be engaged and he would make an honest woman out of her.

Oscar continued to manically stare at Rebecca, and he began envisioning a sick and twisted encounter with the young woman.

She became uncomfortable when she noticed Oscar was relentlessly staring at her with no deviation or divergence.

He was enthralled and couldn't break his mental captivation with her.

When she noticed Oscar's relentless twisted stare, she became extremely uncomfortable, however this was different from the usual attention she often got from the detained low lifes and riff raff of the court that were constantly eyeing her.

Oscar took things to a new perverted level, and so she just uncomfortably continued on with her preparations, confident that she was protected by the armed US Marshals who were positioned all around the courtroom.

Suddenly the court clerk burst out through the judge's chamber door and entered the courtroom!

"The Judge has rendered his decision and will be returning shortly to the courtroom!" the Clerk shouted

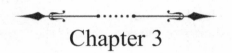

Chapter 3

Outside the courthouse, the area was full of suspense and dreary energy, and all eyes across the nation were focused on the Denver courthouse.

There was a carnival-like atmosphere surrounding the courthouse and the streets were occupied by thousands of people, and scores of protesters who were carrying on about all sorts of grievances.

None really had much to do with Oscar, however if there were TV cameras present, people suddenly had a cause.

There were hundreds of vendors scattered throughout the streets, selling food, drinks and souvenirs.

The tee shirt vendors were peddling their crude and sickly humorous T-shirts to the thousands of people congregating outside the courthouse.

One vendor was selling "Slam Dunk!" T-shirts with a cartoon image of Oscar soaring through the air and slam dunking his mothers head into a basketball hoop!

And another was selling shirts with an image of Oscar dressed as a Harlem Globetrotter spinning his grimacing, hacked off parents' heads on the ends of his pointer fingers.

As distasteful as they were, they were selling out like hot cakes.

There were hundreds of television satellite trucks lined up and down the streets, and herds of reporters were there interviewing the pedestrians and bystanders, questioning them whether or not they thought Oscar deserved to be released.

The consensus was that most believed that he should definitely stay locked up, but incredibly there were several women who were off their rockers and in love with Oscar.

They stated that he should be released and that they wanted to marry Oscar, but if not then conjugal visits would be sufficient with them.

One reporter sarcastically replied;

"Sounds like you already lost your head over this guy."

In the distance, the crowd began to part as a large black SUV, which was escorted by a flashing police cruiser, was directed to a location next to the courthouse and it parked on a narrow side street parallel to the building.

A small group exited the car and were escorted into the courthouse by several US Marshals.

They just so happened to be the immediate family of the murdered Tracy Fernadez and Oscar's Aunt Mary and Uncle Ned, who were presently handling Oscar's parents estate.

If Oscar was to be returned to prison, all the estates assets which were valued over $43 million (including Oscar's parents home), would be turned over to Ned, since he was all that was left of their family, other than Oscar.

Otherwise, ironically if Oscar is set free, the entire massive estate had to be relinquished back to Oscar,

who, due to his own horrendous and egregious actions, just happened to be the only surviving member in his immediate family, and was the only beneficiary to his parents estate.

Unfortunately for his Uncle Ned and Aunt Mary, they would get nothing in that case, so it was in their best interest if Oscar lost his appeal and was returned back to prison.

The two families were there to put pressure on the judge as a last ditch effort to lock up Oscar and throw away the key, forever.

Oscar's life was now in the hands of a judge.

A stranger who didn't even know him, who held his future in the palm of his hands.

No one, not even his parents could understand how a pure and innocent child born into a house full of love and kindness, could progress into the sick perverted person that Oscar had evolved into.

There was nothing unusual about his mothers pregnancy, other than that even in the womb, Oscar was a tumultuous fetus.

Always active and kicking, she hardly got any sleep.

But what other factors really contribute to determine a person's path in life other than their environment?

The only other conclusion may be that they are born that way. It's innate from the start. Their DNA is corrupt, and the wires in their brains are plugged into the wrong circuits.

Their impulses and thoughts are deviant, and they are born without the normal feelings of love, kindness and compassion.

Instead they are left with warped psychopathic feelings such as coldness, hate, impulsiveness, lack of remorse and lack of empathy.

And worst of all, they are deranged and violent.

Who can say whether Oscar ever had a chance at a normal life with his enlarged brain organs.

What contributing factors make a person either a genius or a philanthropist?

Why are some so passionate about doing good things for people and working to benefit society, while psychopaths thrive on the converse and crave to do harm and wreak havoc?

Was there ever such a creature as a psychopath who was a serial do-gooder? Someone who had no remorse about stalking people and killing them with kindness and generosity?

Showering human beings and animals with love and compassion.

No, it's always the same old thing.

Anger, hate, torture, murder and sick and perverted mutilation.

That's the norm, and that's what Oscar is, and what others like him are.

Sick and disgusting creatures that the only benefit to society is that they are locked up and off the streets, hopefully forever.

No treatment could ever rehabilitate him, other than a much stronger dose of electroshock therapy, such as the electric chair, was ever going to save the world from Oscar.

Even the anti-capital punishment protesters who picketed outside on the streets, didn't have a good

argument why someone like Oscar should be left to spend any time on this Earth.

The tension in the courtroom was robust, and there was extreme intensity in the courthouse hallways, which were packed with camera crews and reporters.

There were several courtroom "runners" that were racing back and forth, reporting to the crowd of reporters and the thousands of bystanders outside the courthouse, who were pushing their way through the hordes of cameras and reporters hoping to catch a glimpse of Oscar.

Suddenly, out of nowhere the court Clerk charged out from the judge's chamber and made another announcement;

"Ladies and gentlemen, order in the court! Please take your seats and become silent and remain seated. Make no disruptions. There shall be no shouting or outbursts, either before or after the verdict is announced, or you may be at risk of being held and charged with "Contempt of court" and you will be escorted out of the courthouse and locked up in the county jail. The Judge will be entering the court in a matter of minutes with his decision."

The spectators in the courtroom instantly rushed to find their seats, and they eagerly settled down as they nervously anticipated the Judge's ultimate decision.

Oscar continued on with his relentless perverted fixation on Rebecca, as the courtroom hustled around him.

He seemed to lose focus of the magnitude of the judges decision, and how it would affect his future.

In his mind, nothing else mattered beyond this immediate moment and his twisted fixation and fatal attraction to Rebecca.

He was a blood thirsty lion who was stalking an unsuspecting gazelle, and he had no concern or consciousness of what else was in his way. Nothing else mattered to him, but the kill.

Rebecca sat quietly and continued on ignoring his sadistic gaze, but it was becoming extremely uncomfortable for her until finally, one of the US Marshals became aware of it, and walked over to him and slapped him across the face!

"Knock it off, Demento!!" he sternly reprimanded Oscar.

It was his old nemesis US Marshal Djokovitch who after all those years, was still working at the courthouse.

"Don't make me drag your punk ass outside again, Oscar!" the Marshal scolded.

Oscar seemed to momentarily snap out of his perverted fixation with the girl, but then he began to swell and he clenched his arms as they were constrained in his straight jacket!

His adrenalin began to surge and he was becoming unhinged from the Marshal's slap.

However, it took all of Oscar's concentration and fortitude to settle down and not break through his restraints.

He could have easily ripped the straight jacket to pieces and broken his shackles, but that surely would have gotten him thrown back in jail and charged with assault and battery, and possibly murder.

No, Oscar wanted out, and he knew the US Marshal was baiting him into a confrontation, to be returned to prison.

The Clerk suddenly entered the courtroom and stood at attention, and then made an announcement;

"All Rise!!" and then suddenly the Judge burst into the courtroom from his chamber.

He was wearing a long black judges robe which trailed behind him due to his confident and swift gait, and he was carrying a thick brown legal folder under his arm.

In a flurry he quickly charged up to his bench and sat down harshly on his black leather chair and he rolled it back into place.

He prepared himself, and then he put on his glasses and removed his documents from his valise, and then he briskly took hold of his gavel and slammed it down on his desk top!

"Ladies and Gentleman of the court, I have reached my decision!"

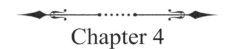

Chapter 4

The courtroom reporters and bystanders were extremely anxious, and there was a loud clamor of chatter in the courtroom.

The judge became angry and slammed his gavel down 5 more times until the courtroom was silenced.

Everyone was stunned by the loud banging and they quickly settled down and became silent.

The judge then began to speak;

"I will have no more of this disrespectful conduct in my courtroom! This was a highly contentious court hearing and I expect to have silence, peace and order when I reveal my verdict! There will be no shouting out or atrocious conduct. Everyone shall remain seated until after my verdict is read, and I exit the courtroom. Anyone who disregards my warnings shall be held in contempt of court and be promptly delivered to the county jail for no less than two days. My perception was that the clerk had already made that clear prior to my entry, and I expect you all to abide by my terms."

The judge continued;

"Bailiff, will you please assist the defendant to rise and stand."

The bailiff walked over and lifted Oscar up from his chair.

Oscar was unsteady and unable to rise on his own since his arms were constrained by a straight jacket, and his legs were tightly shackled with chains.

The judge then began sifting through his file binder of legal paperwork until he found the document he was looking for, and he handed it to the court clerk to certify.

The clerk briefly reviewed the document and seemed stoic as he turned and walked the document over to another table, and handed it to the court secretary to be recorded.

The Clerk waited patiently as the secretary recorded the judgment in the official trial binder and then she handed the document back to the Clerk who then returned it back to the judge.

The Judge took hold of the document and began to clear his throat as the entire courtroom was quiet and in a state of dire suspense.

And then the judge spoke to the court;

"Oscar Lawrence Dimento, this hearing was initiated due to your appeal, of that which, you were being incarcerated for the quadruple homicide of your family members, for which you committed when you were just a juvenile more than eight years ago, and for the murder of your teacher at the psychiatric facility, when you were at the age of 11 and a half.

This hearing is, and what this is based on today, which is your affirmation of your constitutional rights and of that, that you are a legal citizen of the state of Colorado and over the age of eighteen.

The Colorado legal statute asserts that any child over the age of 12 can be prosecuted as an adult. Since Mr. Demento's first felony violation took place

when he was at the tender young age of 10 and then his second felony violation at eleven and a half years of age, during both incidents he was well below the legal statute of adult prosecution, and was at that time directed or was already residing at the Colorado Mental Health Institute (CMHI) at Pueblo. Which is the only facility in the state that was designed to house deviant psychopaths and the criminally insane.

I do believe that it was gross negligence on behalf of the facilities staff to release him into the hands of the ADMAX prison facility in Florence. However, be that as it may, it was done and he was technically "released" from the CMHI facility.

There were no provisions in place from your initial or previous hearings, regarding whether or not you would be confined to the CMHI Pueblo facility indefinitely or for any duration of time for that matter.

The doctors there say you are a threat to society and should be locked up, and that you are a dangerous and deranged psychopath. But what exactly is "dangerous?" Is it a personality characteristic such as a temper or a sense of humor? Or is it something innate and that some might just be born that way. We all have aggressive and destructive thoughts and urges. It's a common human emotion which is rarely acted upon, and less than often ever leads to psychopathic or violent acts. On the other hand it does happen, and that's why our correction facilities are full to capacity.

Now, here I am, a judge, duly obligated to enforce the laws of the State of Colorado. The law clearly decrees in the State of Colorado's constitutional bylaws that 'no minor, unless tried as an adult, shall

be incarcerated for not longer than his or her eighteenth birthday, and with that, all their previous juvenile records shall be expunged and destroyed'.

And furthermore, once a patient is released from any hospital by their acting physician(s), albeit physical injury or mental illness, it must be construed that they are well.

Mr. Dimento was legally released from the Pueblo institution, and then later passed his mental competency exam. Although bound by these legal loopholes, I must pass judgment without prejudice.

Therefore it is my judgement, that you Oscar Lawrence Dimento, shall be emancipated immediately, and your records be expunged and destroyed, and so you shall have no record of your previous violent history and you are leaving here with a clean slate going forward.

I suggest you take this new beginning to heart and focus on doing good and charitable things with your massive inheritance that will benefit society. My advice to you is to stay out of trouble and continue getting psychiatric help.

If I ever see you in my court again, I'll make damn sure you never ever see the light of day again! God help us..."

The judge turned his direction to the stunned and paralyzed US Marshals, and directed them to remove Oscars restraints.

The court runners fled the courtroom shouting out that;

"Oscar is Free!!"

Marshal Djokevitch, who had just previously slapped Oscar across the face, was now forced to bow

down before him and remove his restraints, as Oscar smugly stood over him and laughed.

"See ya around, Marshal Joke-o-vitch," Oscar sarcastically and maliciously stated, as he stretched his arms and legs and locked his devious stare on him.

Despite the judge's warnings, the crowd erupted and everyone stormed out of the courtroom.

The reporters and television crews were rushing out in all directions to be the first to break the news that Oscar was now a free man.

Oscar took a deep breath and was somewhat in a state of jubilant shock, and as he turned to exit the courtroom, he was inundated by reporters.

Everyone wanted a statement from Oscar, but he was overwhelmed and so he pushed through the crowd and exited the court house.

There was a microphone podium set up near the courthouse doors which was surrounded by dozens of reporters, and they shouted out for a statement from Oscar.

He approached the podium and stood there with his simple mind, searching for words when he suddenly noticed Rebecca, the court stenographer leaving the courthouse through a side door.

He visually tracked her as she walked to her small compact car parked in the court employee parking lot, and from a distance, he instantly noticed her vanity license plate which spelled out her name, "REBECCA".

When the herd of reporters shouted out once again for a statement, and what he was going to do with his life? All he chillingly stated was;

"I'm going to Disneyland," and he abruptly left the podium and was quickly escorted off by a police officer into an awaiting squad car, where he was to be transported back to his parents home.

Marshal Djokovitch approached him as he sat in the back seat of the cruiser, and the police officer started the car.

"I'll be watching you, you psycho pervert piece of shit! Every second, every minute, every hour, everywhere you go. Whatever you do, my eyes will be on you! Just give me a simple reason to blow your brains out, and it'll be all over for you, and your sick and useless life!" firmly stated Marshal Djokovitch.

Oscar stuck out his tongue and pressed his face tightly against the glass window and made a maniacal, hideous face as he taunted the Marshal, and then he just chuckled as he comfortably relaxed in the back seat of the cruiser, and the police officer slowly drove off through the crowded street, heading to his mansion in Littleton, about 10 miles west of Denver.

As he sat there riding in the back of the police car, he wasn't reveling in his new found freedom, or the fact that he was now wealthy and he had cheated the system.

No, now he was obsessed with only one thing in his deranged mind...Rebecca.

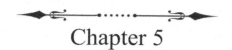

Chapter 5

Officer Laredo, who was the police officer driving the cruiser, was silent during the drive back to Oscar's homestead in Littleton.

They were initially being followed by several paparazzi, but the police officer drove through several red lights with his flashing police lights and siren blaring and was able to lose them.

However, when they finally arrived at Oscar's home, there were dozens of reporters and television crews lined up and down his street, and they had encircled the entrance to his driveway.

The crowd reluctantly parted as the police cruiser was slowly turning into the cobblestone entrance, and it slowly proceeded up the tall hedge lined driveway.

And from that point on into the property, it was impossible to be seen from the road.

The estate was meticulously well groomed and well kept, despite the fact that the house had been empty for the past 8 years.

Oscar's Uncle Ned made sure that the property was well maintained and magnificent considering he expected to be the one to inherit it, along with the massive amount of money included in his brother's estate, once Oscar was out of the way for good.

The tiny stones crackled under the police cruiser's tires as the car slowly rolled along its path up the driveway, and it traveled around a circle until the

cruiser finally stopped under the portico, attached to the front of the house's main entrance.

Oscar sat quietly as Officer Laredo remained smugly in his seat.

"Get out freak, your free ride is over!" ordered Officer Laredo.

The officer then picked up his radio handset and reported to the police station that squad car #795 had delivered the passenger and he would be returning back to the Denver police station shortly after he took his supper break, and then he ended his statement with a "code 10-4".

Oscar tried to get out by opening the door, but the door handle was inoperable and the door wouldn't open.

He instantly realized that the rear doors of the police cruiser were designed to only open from the outside, so that the rear seat occupants or prisoners were locked in and could not escape.

"Excuse me, Officer Loredo, you're gonna have to let me out of the car, this handle doesn't work," Oscar simply stated.

The police officer laughed and then began to heckle Oscar.

"You're not going anywhere you psychotic asshole! Did you actually think we were going to turn you loose into our city with that twisted demonic brain of yours? You didn't fool anyone by faking your test answers on that PCL test, and now you're going to have a little "freak" accident!" the police officer jeered.

Oscar was beginning to panic as he began desperately yanking on the door handle, with no success!

"Sorry Oscar, you're going to have to die. Besides, your Uncle Ned made a huge contribution to my retirement fund so he can cash in on your inheritance. You taking the hit is a win-win for everyone!" chuckled the officer.

The police officer then exited the cruiser and opened up his trunk, where he removed a long flexible corrugated hose and a roll of duct tape.

He slipped one end of the hose over the end of the police car's exhaust pipe and the other end into the driver side window, which he left narrowly open, and duct taped the remaining gap closed, completely sealing the window.

Oscar's heart rate began to vigorously increase as gray smoke began billowing into the police car.

The noxious smell of carbon monoxide and smoke began saturating the compartment and it began to overwhelm him.

His heart rate intensified as his brain reacted, and it began releasing massive amounts of adrenaline into his bloodstream!

The police officer leaned back against the front fender of the squad car and lit up a cigarette as he waited for Oscar to succumb and die from carbon monoxide poisoning.

It was a scheme carefully devised with the assistant coroner, who would state that Oscar had passed away from a brain aneurysm brought on by the site of his old homestead.

Oscar was suddenly beyond his boiling point and began kicking at the locked car door.

With every kick the door wrinkled and expanded outward and by the third kick, he completely broke the door off its hinges!

He quickly took hold of the dismantled car door and charged at the officer, using it as a large metallic shield.

The panic stricken officer, instantly realizing he was in big trouble, drew his pistol and shot his entire bullet clip at Oscar, point blank!

But Oscar was quickly upon him, and he smashed the steel door into the officer, knocking him fiercely across the driveway and to the ground!

In a full blown psychotic rage, Oscar viciously continued beating the man senseless while quarts of adrenaline continued to pump throughout his veins.

During his brutal assault, Oscar easily overpowered the officer, and he pummeled and mauled him incessantly, as if he were a mad rabid dog released from its cage.

Officer Laredo was unconscious and barely alive when Oscar finally stopped his onslaught.

Oscar then turned his nose up to the air and began sniffing and drawing in the perspiration and body odor that was emitting from the unconscious policeman, and then he crouched down into a hideous monkey walk pose and began scurrying about on all fours, and whooping it up as if he were an excited chimp.

He effortlessly dragged the officer's distorted body by his limp arm, up the brick staircase which led to

the front door, and yanked him through the doorway into his old home.

He then stripped Officer Laredo out of his uniform, and dragged him into the dining room where he tossed him recklessly on top of the polished mahogany table.

As Officer Laredo was helplessly lying there, Oscar was becoming sexually charged and he began tearing off his blood splattered prison uniform until he was completely naked, and then he began fondling himself and whooping it up grunting once again in his ape chatter.

Oscar was only getting started, and needed more to satisfy his sadistic craving, and so he quickly left the policeman and monkey trotted directly into the garage where he found his old butcher's cleaver and hunting knife, exactly where he had hidden them 8 years ago, behind one of the old storage cabinets.

When he returned, he noticed that the officer had rolled off the dining room table and was desperately trying to escape by crawling towards the front door.

Oscar once again became enraged and dragged him back into the dining room and slammed him back down on top of the table.

He then began stabbing the officer mercilessly with his hunting knife, and then he climbed up and squatted on top of him and began chopping though his rib cage with his cleaver!

Once he broke through, he then carved out his heart with his massive hunting knife as Officer Laredo laid there dead and eviscerated on top of the dining room table!

As Oscar held his heart, it continued to beat in his hand, and then he manically began rubbing the pulsing blood all over his face and tasted the blood.

He was about to return to Officer Laredo's body, to completely gut him when there was an unexpected knock on the back door.

Oscar scampered over with his hideous monkey trot to a rear window, while still carrying his butcher's cleaver in one hand and the pulsing heart in the other, and saw that there was a man standing there at the back door, holding a briefcase in one hand and a thick manilla envelope in the other.

He instantly recognized the man, it was his dear Uncle Ned who was obviously there to pay off the policeman for his service.

Oscar quickly trotted over and aggressively swung the back door open, shocking the living hell out of his Uncle Ned, who had already presumed that by now, Oscar was dead.

"Hi Unkie, Come on in we're having a dinner party!! Officer Laredo is already waiting for us at the dining room table!" Oscar manically stated.

Oscar then took a bite of the police officer's pulsing heart just as if it were a juicy red apple, and then aggressively grabbed his uncle by his necktie and yanked him inside, slamming the door shut behind him with his foot!

Instantly his uncle took notice of Oscar's wild eyes and that he was totally naked, and his face and body were saturated in blood!

And then he noticed the trail of blood splatter on the floor and walls, leading into the dining room, and through the doorway he could barely see the end of

the dining room table where the police officer's mutilated body was lying there, gutted on top of the dining room table.

"Oscar, what have you done?!! You were just set free with a clean slate less than a few hours ago, and with an enormous fortune to do whatever you pleased! WHY!!" shouted his uncle.

Oscar grinned and replied;

"Haven't you ever heard the tale of the Turtle and the Scorpion, Uncle Ned?" Oscar manically questioned.

His uncle nervously shook his head realizing the horrific predicament he was in.

"Uh, no Oscar, I haven't," he fearfully responded.

Oscar continued;

"A turtle was resting on a water bank when a scorpion approached him and asked him for a ride across the pond. The turtle responded that he would not give him a ride across the pond, because he was a deadly scorpion and he would fatally sting him once he was on his back.

The scorpion replied;

"I am a kind and gentle scorpion unlike all the others, and besides, if I were to do that, I would surely drown and die too!"

And so the kind hearted turtle decided to help and give the scorpion a ride on his back across the pond.

Minutes later, when they were half way across the pond, and at the pond's deepest point, the scorpion unleashed his venomous stinger into the turtle's neck!

The turtle was stunned by the scorpion's egregious action as he felt the poison rushing into his body and paralysis was setting in!

The scorpion laughed as the turtle began to sink and he struggled to stay afloat.

The turtle then desperately uttered;

"How could you have done this to me after I was so kind to you, and allowed you to ride on my back, and now you will surely drown and die too!"

The scorpion became indifferent and severely stung the turtle a second time and then replied;

"I am a scorpion, and it's my nature to do bad things as irrational as they may seem," but you Uncle Ned, you are a snake who paid to get rid of me to steal my inheritance, and that was not very nice either!" scolded Oscar.

His uncle desperately turned and tried to open the door to escape, but Oscar swung his butcher's cleaver and stuck it directly into the center of his spine, and then he continued the onslaught and began chopping him to pieces as if he were an oak tree, until he finally hit the ground!

His uncle, barely alive, attempted to claw his way across the floor as he screamed in horrific agony.

But Oscar was super charged and relentless.

He dragged him into the dining room and tossed him up onto the dining room table and planted him right next to the dead officer's body.

Oscar was in his maniacal psychopathic zone now, and after so many years of pent up frustration, and his inability to satisfy his need to torture and kill, he was now fulfilling and satisfying his deranged psychopathic hunger.

And so he began to shout;

"Oscar Dimento took an axe and gave the Policeman 400 whacks, and when he had found out

what his uncle had done, he gave his Uncle Ned 401!"

Oscar continued his hideous chant over and over, as he obliterated his uncle with his bloody cleaver and then too, carved out his pulsating heart.

Finally, Oscar dragged the two hollow masses of mangled flesh into the kitchen and propped them up on the kitchen chairs and let them fold over and collapse onto the kitchen table.

He opened a cabinet and took notice of his old cartoon cup of "The Joker", his villainous mentor from the Batman series, and filled it with cold water from the sink.

He scuttled over and then sat down at the head of the table, sipping water from his nefarious cup, as he made small talk with his dead and mutilated guests.

"So, Officer Laredo, would you like a drink of water, or do you think it will go right through you?!" Oscar chuckled as he waited for the dead officer to respond.

"How about you Uncle Ned, would you like to play catch with Officer Laredo's gonads? Whoever drops them first is a monkey's uncle!" Oscar bellowed out.

Oscar continued on with his one sided conversation, but quickly became frustrated that his company was lacking edicate and being rude by not responding to his gentlemanly chit chat about the weather and the traffic on the way back to Littleton, and so he excused himself and began roaming around the house in his 'monkey' romp, when he noticed the new carpeting in the living room.

It was installed by his uncle to replace the old carpeting that was there before, the one that was

soaked with his family's blood after he slaughtered them all.

He began sniffing the area as if he were a bloodhound, and making subtle ape sounds, and then he suddenly tore back the carpet revealing a huge dark burgundy stain embedded into the subfloor below, and the site of the stain excited him.

He began hopping up and down and whooping it up, as if he were a frantic ape and then threw himself down onto the blood stain, rolling himself over it to gather the scent of his family's blood.

He then noticed the staircase which led to the upstairs bedrooms, and he paused and sniffed the air, and something drew him over to it.

He crept down low like a spider, and with his belly to the ground he began crawling up the staircase, and up to his old bedroom.

He noticed that the hasp locks that were once used to lock him in his room were now gone, however the holes in the wood from the screws were apparent and just recklessly painted over.

As he entered his old bedroom, there was a musty smell and it was completely empty.

He saw that the room had been painted and all the holes and broken plaster had been repaired except for the inside of his bedroom door that was still battered and disfigured from all the times when he was trying to escape from his room and fiercely tried to get through the door.

He then made his way into his parent's bedroom, still maintaining his hideous monkey trot, and he sprang up onto their bed and began sniffing at their musty pillows and linens.

He circled around on top of their bed several times as if he was searching for a good spot, then he lifted his leg as a dog would and urinated on their pillows, and then he sprang off and defecated in the corner of their room.

He continued on, roaming on all fours, and trotted into their master bathroom and began filling the bathtub.

He delicately tested the water temperature several times until he finally crawled in and submerged himself without ever shutting the water off, and let it overflow the tub as he enjoyed his bath.

He sank down several times under the water, washing the blood splatter off while pretending to be dead until his attention quickly shifted to the medicine cabinet over the bathroom sink, and he crawled out of the overflowing tub.

He approached the bathroom sink and opened the medicine cabinet and stood there staring at its contents. It was mostly empty except for his father's razor knife.

He carefully opened it and gazed at it as he began running his finger up and down its long flat silvery blade.

He curiously placed the blade against his face and carefully shaved off his orange scraggly beard.

He nicked himself several times and got some sort of sick pleasure from watching blood dripping off of his face and into the sink.

He then rinsed his face and then combed his long shoulder length bright red hair, and then tied it into a ponytail with one of his mothers old hair ties.

He then left the bathroom, naked with a towel over his shoulders and then sauntered down the staircase and returned back to the kitchen.

"You guys still here? I thought maybe you wanted to count your money and run," Oscar snickered as he again maintained his monkey trot and hopped up onto the kitchen table and squatted, trying to relieve himself into an empty fruit bowl.

"Sorry guys, I guess I'm empty!" Oscar chuckled and he sprang off the table as if he were some sort of mangy squirrel.

He trotted back into the foyer where he found Officer Laredo's uniform cast about, and it interested him.

And so he began deeply sniffing and poking at it, as if he were an interested primate in the jungle who had stumbled on a human being's rubbish.

His curiosity continued, and so he began licking and tasting the officer's perspiration from the cloth.

Then, Oscar had an idea, and so he began picking up the articles of clothing and dressed himself in Officer Laredo's wrinkled uniform, until he was completely outfitted as a police officer.

Lastly, he attached the utility belt with the empty gun holster.

He looked into the foyer mirror and was impressed with himself, but noticed some things were missing. His butcher's cleaver and hunting knife.

He returned to the dining room and gathered his cutlery, as a mechanic or wood worker would pick up their tools.

Emboldened with his new outfit he went outside and found the officer's spent gun and placed it back

into its holster, and picked up his crumpled policeman's hat, and then carefully corrected it and he nobly placed it on his head.

"There, now that's better," he manically thought.

Oscar then removed the long corrugated hose from the car's exhaust pipe and then pulled the other duct taped end of the hose from the driver's window and opened the door and turned off the engine.

He waited there several minutes, until the smoke had cleared and the fumes were gone, and then he curiously climbed in and sat in the driver seat.

In his psychopathic and demented mind he looked things over, and thought it would be fun to turn on the police cars flashing blue lights and sirens, but first he picked up the police radio handset and pushed in the button.

"One Adam 12, This is car #795. I need to run a license plate, 10-4".

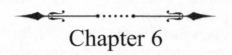

Chapter 6

Rebecca was late for her church choir practice, mainly because of the heavy downtown traffic due to the trial.

After she finally parked her car in the church's parking lot, she then rushed to enter the church.

The grand and massive pipe organs were blaring and echoing throughout the large and open hall, as the organist was warming up her hands for the choir's practice.

Rebecca stopped and closed her eyes as she drew in the thunderous tones.

She loved the church and the sound of the pipe organ, as it gave her sanity in this mixed up world.

She was very religious and spent most of her life at the church, since her father was also the church's minister.

As she approached the grand podium she stood before a giant crucifix which was mounted high above and behind the minister's platform.

Her father was there preparing for that evening's service, and he stopped when he saw her and gave her a warm hug.

She noticed that the other choir members were already there and congregating on the right side of the stage, and were waiting for her and a few others to arrive so that they could begin practice.

Something came over her and rather than join her friends, she knelt down before the cross and began to pray.

She had just left the courthouse and was worried about the safety of the people and children of Denver.

Oscar was now free and on the loose, and could cause them harm.

She prayed deeply for the people and their families, and even for Oscar, that he would be healed and his mind would be at peace.

She ended her prayer by thanking Jesus for sending Charlie to her, and for Charlie's love and patience, in that she was taught that she must remain a virgin and celibate until they were married, and Charlie had accepted that.

She ended her prayer by making the sign of the cross across her chest and then quickly joined her choir group.

Charlie had just walked into the church and noticed Rebecca's long blonde hair and her beautiful smile, as he took his place next to his beloved Rebecca up on the choir platform, and they held hands as the pipe organ began bellowing out "Morning has broken".

They frequently gazed at each other as they sang together, not just as two people who were deeply in love, but as soulmates who cherished the fact that they would be together forever.

They were two kind hearted and generous souls, who were totally devoted to Christ and each other.

After singing their final song "Hallelujah," Charlie and Rebecca again took a moment to pray before the grand crucifix, before having a few refreshments that the church had provided.

Rebecca leaned in and sensuously whispered to Charlie that she had a surprise for him tonight.

She revealed that she was ready to give herself to him, even though they were not married yet.

She whispered that she was so in love with him, and that he was her soulmate, and she could not envision giving herself to any other man than him.

Charlie was extremely taken aback and excited to hear that news, considering they have been together for the past 2 ½ years, and he was ready after their very first date.

He graciously looked up at the Crucifix and shouted;

"Thank you, Jesus!!" at the top of his lungs.

Rebecca laughed and was a bit embarrassed as she noticed some of the other choir members taking notice, but she knew that they had no clue what Charlie was referring to.

"Let's go have a romantic dinner out, and then we can go back home and consummate our love," Rebecca romantically stated.

Just then it hit him. Charlie remembered that he had to return to work and finish inventory at the drugstore immediately, so that his boss, Mr. Maxwell could place an order for prescription drugs the following morning!

"Uhggg, I'm so sorry Rebecca, I have to work tonight, but, but I'll be home before 8 o'clock. How about if I pick up some Chinese takeout, and we can have our romantic dinner at home, when I get back?" Charlie pleaded.

Rebecca smiled, and said that she would be there waiting for him, and that she would be completely

naked, only wearing a sheer pink negligee and shaking up a can of whipped cream.

Charlie began to perspire with anticipation and swallowed hard as this long awaited trist was suddenly unfolding before him.

"Should I pick up some strawberries for dessert?" Charlie nervously joked.

And Rebecca lustfully replied;

"You're gonna be my desert, Charlie," and she seductively winked at him.

What Rebecca didn't know was that Charlie had a secret.

After work, he was actually meeting another woman that night.

She worked in the jewelry store where Charlie had been secretly paying off a beautiful diamond engagement ring for Rebecca.

The ring was finally paid off and he had planned on picking it up that evening, after work.

Now that Rebecca had revealed that she was going to give herself to him, there was no better time than that evening to propose to her, immediately after they consummate their love for each other.

Charlie could barely keep the secret, as he caressed her soft blonde hair and fell into her deep blue eyes, as he was entranced by her beauty.

He was the luckiest man on Earth, and this was going to be the best night ever, and a night that neither of them would ever forget!

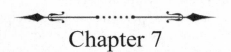

Chapter 7

It was utter chaos at the police station at the end of the day.

It was nearly 6 o'clock and because of all the tumult downtown over the Oscar Demento trial, the police department was understaffed.

It was also supper time, which meant that the changing of shifts had begun, and officers and staff were quickly coming and going.

The dispatch agent was spent after having received hundreds of bogus calls from worried and panic stricken Denver residents with supposed "Oscar sightings".

Everyone had heard the verdict, and was on edge now that Oscar was released and free to roam the streets of Denver.

She was tired, and anxious to leave when she noticed that her police officer boyfriend had just entered the dispatch room, and was waving at her to hurry up, as they were going to be late for their evening bowling league.

As she quickly began gathering her things, suddenly a radio call came in from a police cruiser.

She hesitated when she noticed that her "tramp" shift replacement had just then casually sauntered into the dispatch room, and because her co-worker was late and not at her post yet, she was obligated to take the call.

"One Adam 12, this is car #795. I need to run a license plate, 10-4"

The dispatch agent was distracted and noticed that her sexually aggressive co-worker was now openly flirting with her boyfriend, and she became flustered.

She wasn't at all amused by the sarcastic "One Adam 12" intro line to the call in, since she had heard it hundreds of times before from some of the cops who were still living out of the 1970's.

"Go ahead 795," she hastily responded.

"Colorado plate, 'R-E-B-E-C-C-A' " the male voice stated over the radio.

She began typing in the information into the massive database, and was seething as she was observing her co-worker aggressively "hitting" on her boyfriend.

And so, she totally disregarded the fact that the officer's radio request was completely out of protocol and not done the proper way that it should have been called into the station.

"That tag belongs to a Miss. Rebecca Kannon #2673 Pine St, Aurora. No priors. 10-4."

And then she resentfully shouted out to her counterpart to "Knock it off!" and gave her the deadly "Don't you dare mess with my man" look of death, and then she abruptly left her post at the dispatch station and took hold of her boyfriend's arm and quickly swaggered away.

Oscar now had Rebecca's address, and nothing was going to stop him from getting to her.

The problem was, Oscar had never driven a car before, but knew the basics from watching his parents when he was a kid.

He noticed the two petals on the floor, and when he pushed the petal on the right, the car accelerated and when he pressed the petal on the left, he could feel the brakes engage.

He found the switch which turned on the flashing police car lights, and he played with the sirens a bit, and it excited him.

But then he realized that the loud noise brought too much attention towards him and so he shut them off.

He then took hold and carefully moved the transmission lever into the #1 position, and the car began to slowly roll down the driveway.

He quickly discovered that #1 was a slow gear and so he moved it up to #2 as he approached the end of his driveway.

The massive crowd of reporters had finally left and there was no one there to notice that he was impersonating a police officer, and driving a police car with the rear door blown out.

He began to manically think about Rebecca, and once again became obsessed with her.

He thought about her long blonde hair and her beautiful face and petite figure.

He was on the prowl, and he felt a primitive animalistic need to mate with her.

Oddly, it wasn't a need for sex, or love.

A psychopath like Oscar doesn't have feelings like that.

But rather a more instinctual powerful need to procreate.

Just as animals or insects who cross paths in the wild might do, such as a Black Widow spider or a

Praying Mantis who breed, then murder their mates immediately after copulation.

That's how Oscar perceived it.

Oscar was cautiously making his way through Littleton, recklessly driving and plowing through stop signs and red traffic lights.

However, the other vehicles were actually moving out of his way when they saw a police cruiser with its lights flashing, as if it was on route to some sort of an emergency.

When he finally reached the nearby district of Aurora, he was lost, but noticed a vagrant homeless person, panhandling for money in the middle of the street, and asked him if he knew where Pine Street was.

The man replied that he did in fact know where Pine Street was, since that was near to where his own house was, and then he instantly realized that he had just spilled the beans that he wasn't actually a homeless man, but a con man.

The man nervously continued on with the directions as Oscar picked up Officer Laredo's violation pad and in sarcastic disgust, scribbled out a $500 ticket for panhandling and handed it to the vagrant, and then tipped his hat and drove off.

It didn't take long before Oscar stumbled onto the street, and he pulled over and parked the disfigured police car in front of #2673 Pine Street.

He turned off the flashing lights and then the car's engine and began to intensely concentrate.

He had to control his adrenaline output and calm down, otherwise he might just run in and kill Rebecca before he had the opportunity to mate with her.

As he began to regain some composure, he left the car and tidied himself up a bit.

He tucked his butcher's cleaver and hunting knife behind his back, under his utility belt, and then fixed his hat as he approached the steps going up to the front porch.

As he marched up the stairs his heart began to race again, and he was losing control as he began anticipating his encounter with Rebecca.

His psychotic thoughts were raging in his brain, as adrenalin began pumping out of his skull.

He was desperately trying to contain himself so that he would be perceived as a legitimate police officer, and to have some bit of composure.

He tapped three times on the front door, and after a minute he heard footsteps coming down from the staircase inside, and were approaching the front door.

He turned his nose up in the air and drew in a deep breath of air through his nasal passages, and tried to catch the scent of his mate.

He impatiently knocked again, only harder, and that's when he heard a female voice singing out to him;

"Just a minute, I'm coming, I just got out of the shower and I'm naked!"

His heart began to pump wildly and sweat began building up on his face as breeding was imminent!

The door slowly creaked open and he was instantly taken aback when he saw that it was not Rebecca, but a wet sultry older woman who opened the door, wearing only a revealing skimpy red satin robe.

It was Rebecca's mother, Mrs. Kannon.

She lustfully pretended to be concerned when she saw the police officer at her front door, as she barely held her robe closed.

"Oh my, did I do something wrong, Officer? Maybe, you should come in and handcuff me," she lewdly chuckled.

Oscar's eyes were swirling around in his head and he was barely able to maintain control as he caught a strong whiff of her sexual pheromonal scent.

"I'm looking for Rebecca Kannon, does she live here?" Oscar grunted out.

"Oh, Rebecca. She's my daughter, but she doesn't live with us anymore. Did "Miss Goodie two shoes" do something wrong?"

Mrs. Kannon inquired.

Then she sensuously looked Oscar up and down, and let her robe slip open a bit;

"My oh my, you are a handsome devil. I've always been attracted to a man in a uniform. Hmmm, I feel like I've seen you before? Have you been on TV or something?" Mrs. Kannon seductively questioned, as she proceeded to swoon over Oscar and touch his face.

Her advance was very assertive, and even Oscar the psychopathic lunatic was finding it uncomfortable.

"No, Mame, I just need to speak to her about something that happened at the courthouse. Can you tell me where she lives?" Oscar questioned through his clenched teeth as he fought to control himself.

Mrs. Kannon was very promiscuous, and didn't realize who this police officer really was, as she was aggressively coming on to him.

She stated that Rebecca lived several blocks down the street at # 645 Cedar Street, and went on to say that Rebecca and her boyfriend Charlie, were living together "in sin", and that they were renting the upstairs of a two family house.

Oscar's skin began to crawl when he heard that there was another man with his mate and he became extremely jealous.

He quickly turned to leave when Mrs. Kannon flirtatiously shouted out;

"Officer, I just made some fresh Lemonade, would you care to come inside for a cold drink? My husband will be gone for a few more hours and I'm awfully lonely," and she let her robe drop completely open, revealing herself to him.

He immediately stopped and then turned back, and he saw that Rebeccas's mother (the minister's wife) was a slut, and she was motioning to him to come in, as she was fondling herself and licking her lips.

Oscar was beside himself and becoming deranged and unhinged!

His primal instinct to breed and reproduce was taking over.

Adrenalin and testosterone were pumping into his bloodstream and he needed to get to Rebecca.

But then, Oscar stopped and thought for a moment.

Tracy Fernandez, his teacher from the mental hospital, she was a slut too, and so were his mother and step sisters.

They were all sluts and had to be dealt with!

He slowly turned back to Mrs. Kannon with a maniacal gaze.

She was licking her inviting lips and wagging her fingers for him to come inside and visit with her.

"Why yes, Mrs. Kannon, I would enjoy an ice cold glass of lemonade, thank you!" replied Oscar, and he marched into her home as she shamelessly clung onto him and began kissing his neck.

As he turned to close the door, he cautiously looked back to see if anyone was watching from the street.

And then, he hideously smiled just like the "Joker" on his childhood cup, as his savage, demonic eyes rolled back into his skull, and he closed the door as Mrs. Kannon ravaged him.

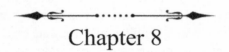

Chapter 8

Charlie had stopped by a flower shop on his way to the jewelry store, and bought a dozen long stem roses, which they placed in a box with a bright red ribbon around it.

He then picked up Rebecca's engagement ring from the jewelry store and was very excited about what the night would bring.

His last stop along the way, he picked up some Chinese takeout food and prepared one of the fortune cookies where he concealed Rebecca's engagement ring inside with a fortune note which read;

"Rebecca, will you marry me?"

It was just minutes before 8 o'clock when Charlie arrived at home and noticed a police cruiser just pulling away from the curb in front of his house, and it quickly exited with its lights flashing.

Charlie drove into the driveway, which ran alongside their house and curved around back, and parked where he always parked, underneath his upstairs bedroom window.

He carefully gathered his things and ecstatically walked around to the front door which led to their upstairs apartment.

He slowly stepped up the stairs, and the old wooden steps softly creaked as he steathfully crept up the steps, trying to be quiet so that he could surprise Rebecca.

He was excited and anticipating the night to come, and couldn't wait to be with her.

Their lives were about to change and it was going to be magnificent. When he finally reached the top of the staircase, he oddly noticed that the entry door into the apartment was ajar and not closed, as if someone had left it open.

He cautiously pushed the door open with his foot as he carried the food and flowers into their apartment and placed them on the kitchen table.

The lights were completely off and it was dark in the house.

As he silently wandered through the rooms, he noticed that their bedroom door was closed.

Something didn't seem right, though.

Rebecca was supposed to be waiting for him with the table set and only wearing her sexy lingerie.

He started to get nervous that maybe she had second thoughts and ran off, or maybe she had some sort of emergency.

But no, that didn't seem logical.

As he approached the bedroom door he was concerned that something might have happened to Rebecca, and so he took hold of the door knob, and slowly turned it while pushing the sticky door open with his knee.

There was a small night light in the room, casting a dim glow and he instantly noticed that Rebecca's clothes were recklessly scattered in front of the doorway.

He cautiously poked his head into the bedroom and saw the silhouette of a seemingly naked and limp

body lying on top of the bed in a contorted position and not moving at all.

Anxiously, he took a few more steps into the room, and saw that something was wrong with Rebecca, and he rushed over to the bed!

Rebecca was lying face down and was unconscious!

Charlie panicked and began to gently shake her and then he tenderly rolled her over when she slowly began to moan, and she opened her eyes.

"I'm sorry Charlie, I fell asleep while I was waiting for you," she softly whispered and she took him in her arms.

They embraced each other and then began passionately kissing and she pulled him closer.

She was only wearing her pink sheer negligee and he began recklessly removing his clothes.

He could feel her body heat pressing against him as they passionately kissed and then began making love.

It was an incredible night as they were both so much in love with each other, and it felt so right.

Afterwards they continued to hold and cuddle each other, and Rebecca began to cry.

Charlie was concerned and asked what was wrong, and she replied;

"I'm just so happy that I have you Charlie," and she tightened her embrace on him.

"I have a surprise for you, my love," Charlie whispered and he began to get out of the bed, and he whispered to her that he would be right back.

He was heading off to the kitchen to get the box of roses, and that special fortune cookie surprise for her.

Oddly, Charlie thought he heard a noise.

It sounded as if their apartment door had opened and then he felt a mild gust of cool air race through into their bedroom and it closed their bedroom door.

He stood there a moment listening intently, and when he considered that he was only being paranoid and nothing was there, he reached for the doorknob, and then suddenly the door exploded into the bedroom and knocked Charlie across the room!

Oscar came crashing in completely naked, like a raging bull swinging his butcher's cleaver in one hand and his hunting knife in the other!

He directed all his rage at Charlie, who was caught off guard and struggling to make sense of what was happening!

Rebecca was screaming hysterically as Oscar attacked Charlie, who was no match against Oscar's powerful rampage, and he was being slashed and hacked to shreds and pounded like a rag doll!

Charlie desperately fought back with all his might, but Oscar finally grabbed hold of him and launched him across the room, and Charlie inadvertently burst out through their 2nd floor window, and he fell aimlessly into the darkness of night until his body came crashing down on top of his car, which was parked below.

He was instantly knocked unconscious as he flattened the roof of his car and was bleeding profusely.

Rebecca continued screaming, and she recognized Oscar!

Now he turned his full attention toward her, and he raised his nose up in the air and deeply drew in the air

through his nostrils as he clung to his cleaver and knife!

The air in the room was heavy with Rebecca's scent, and it drove him into a sexual craze, and he was hungering to mate with her.

She tried hopelessly to get away from him, and she lunged to jump out of the broken window to get away and help Charlie, despite the fact that it was two stories above the ground!

In the moment, she instantly noticed Charlie lying motionless on top of his car in a pool of blood, and covered with broken window glass.

Before she could jump, Oscar dropped his weapons, and grabbed hold of her long blond hair, and then dragged her back to the bed and threw her face down onto the mattress!

He twisted her hair around his fist and slid his other hand under her stomach, as she thrashed aimlessly about, screaming for help and fighting to get away!

He took a deep breath and filled his nostrils with her perfume and began inhaling her venereal scent.

Her smell charged him into a sexually ferocious beast, and so he pulled back on her hair and he hoisted her up by her waist, and manipulated her, and then aggressively mounted and violently raped her, over and over!

Oscar was sexually exhilarated and his eyes were crazed as he viciously carried out his sexual assault on her.

It was brutally violent and Rebecca's screams became silent as her head repeatedly impacted against the bed's solid oak headboard, and she suddenly

became unconscious as Oscar wildly thrusted her back and forth into delirium.

When it was finally over, Oscar released and backed away from her.

He looked at what he perceived as "what she had done" and saw that Rebecca was now soiled, and impure.

In his twisted mind it was her that enticed him and had it coming, now he saw her as a slut that had to be punished.

He turned her over and brutally attacked Rebecca, pounding her face and viciously clawing her breasts as he squatted on top of her.

Oscar, then desperately looked for something to cut her head off with!

He saw his hunting knife that he had dropped on the floor, and so he scrambled off of her and picked it up, and then pressed it against his face, feeling the cold steel against his skin, and he paused for a moment in deep thought.

It was as if he suddenly realized that he himself was the sick psychotic creature and he needed to end his own life, so that Rebecca may live.

He began to buckle over and he cried out to his "Mama" and then he raised the knife to his own throat and drew his arm across his neck to deliver a fatal slash to himself!

Then suddenly he heard a voice in the back of his head.

It was "The Joker" speaking to Oscar in his condescending voice.

"Don't be a pussy, Oscar! Get back in the game and finish that slut off! You are here for a reason, my

boy. To curse the world and kill all the sluts!" The Joker chuckled and hideously laughed.

Oscar lowered his knife and with a new sense of conviction he quickly returned his attention back toward Rebecca.

He crawled up on top of Rebecca's unresponsive body and began licking and tasting her bloody sweat as he once again empowered himself and drew in the aroma of her blood, perspiration, and her body's carnal fragrance into his nostrils.

He recklessly tossed her back over onto her belly and squatted on her naked rump, and wrapped a handful of her long blonde hair around his clenched fist.

He began drawing her head back towards him, stretching her throat back, and arching her spine as he raised her shoulders and mangled breasts off the bed.

He leaned forward and brought the hunting knife across her fully exposed throat, and salivated as he clenched his decayed teeth as he prepared to slice Rebecca's head clean off!!

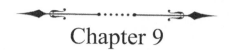

Chapter 9

Marshal Djokovitch was driving his unmarked cruiser home later that evening, after filing a massive amount of paperwork regarding the trial.

It was the end of the day, but he had an uneasy feeling about the whole ordeal.

"How could that homicidal psychopath be out on the streets!" he tragically contemplated.

He had an odd gut feeling that he should drive over to Oscar's house to check on things, just in case there was a problem already.

He also thought that it would be a good idea to let Oscar know that he was watching him, and he better not step out of line.

The Marshal was completely dumbfounded and still couldn't believe that Oscar was released on a technicality, and he literally feared that it wouldn't be long before Oscar snapped, and seriously hurt someone.

He turned his car around and instinctively headed toward Littleton, where Oscar's family home was.

When he arrived at the house and pulled into the driveway, it was quiet and nothing seemed out of place, other than there was a small silver Toyota Camry parked on the grass, awkwardly off the driveway near the back of the house.

The Marshal paused and ran the license plate of the Camry, and he discovered that it was Oscar's Uncle Ned's car, and when he inspected the vehicle, he felt the temperature of the hood.

It was cool and must have been there for a while.

He cautiously continued on foot toward the front entry, where he discovered the bullet riddled and disfigured rear passenger door of a police cruiser.

It was lying awkwardly on the driveway and completely obliterated. There was also a long plastic corrugated hose with some long pieces of duct tape still attached to one end of it, which was cast recklessly off to the side of the driveway.

The Marshal was confused, but one thing was for sure, Oscar had something to do with this, and it seemed that he must have broken himself out of the back seat of the police cruiser, and there were gunshots fired.

Clearly, the abandoned police car door was full of bullet holes and there were spent bullet casings scattered all about, on the driveway.

However, something wasn't right, and it seemed that Officer Laredo, who was driving Oscar home, was up to something with the duct taped hose.

The Marshal then steathfully continued up the steps to the front door with his pistol drawn.

He peered into the window and noticed the house was in disarray and quiet.

He cautiously opened the front door and immediately noticed a trail of blood streaks and splatter that led through the hallways of the house.

As he continued on in, he discovered a broad blood trail which led through the grand entryway into the dining room.

The walls were completely covered with blood splatter and there was a massive amount of blood pooled up, especially under the dining room table, and what seemed to be human organs that were cast all over the room.

When he continued on into the kitchen, it was there where he was mortified and sickened to find a naked Officer Laredo, and Oscar's Uncle Ned butchered and hacked to pieces and perched up onto the kitchen chairs, slumped over and face down on the kitchen table!

He suddenly became faint and a wave of intense nausea overwhelmed him, and so he raced out of the house and fell to his knees on the lawn and began vomiting from the horrific and gruesome sight, and the stench of death that filled the home.

After a few moments he regained his composure and ran over to his cruiser.

He called in to the police station, and reported that Oscar was on the loose and was impersonating a police officer!

"Be on the lookout for a police cruiser with a missing rear door! The officer driving the vehicle is an imposter and it is no other than Oscar Demento! He is armed and extremely dangerous!"

He continued and reported that;

"A gruesome double homicide has taken place at the Demento mansion in Littleton, and the notorious Oscar Demento is the perpetrator!"

He no sooner hung up his radio microphone when another announcement came across the radio,

"Dispatch, calling for any squad car available in the vicinity of #1269 Pine St. Aurora. Husband reports a vicious homicide at the residence."

Instantly the Marshal picked up his radio microphone and inquired the name of the victim.

"Mrs. Marsha Kannon 10-4," replied the dispatcher.

The Marshal had a sinking feeling as he knew instantly what the situation was.

After observing Oscar as he became mesmerized by Rebecca Kannon in the courtroom, it only made sense that he was after her, and somehow her mother got in his way.

He started his car and sped toward the Kannon's house with his sirens blaring!

As he recklessly drove, he had called dispatch again requesting any information on Rebecca Kannon.

The dispatcher replied that it was on record that someone had requested her automobile license plate information approximately two hours earlier, and it was the same address as the homicide at her parents home.

"The victims husband, who is a minister, arrived at the home shortly after the evening mass and discovered his wife's mutilated and dismembered body," the dispatcher reported.

Marshal Djokovich concluded that somehow Oscar had acquired Rebecca's name or her license plate when she left the court house, and called it in using the police cruiser's radio.

On his way to the crime scene, the Marshal noticed he was passing by the Denver zoo where he had a close friend who was the chief veterinarian there.

He quickly pulled into the personnel-only parking lot which was adjacent to the veterinary office, and he charged right into the animal hospital.

There was no one there, but he rummaged through the medicine cabinet and found exactly what he was looking for, a large bottle of Metoprolol. The adrenalin blocking drug.

As he rushed out of the hospital, he took hold of a long rifle case which was in one of the storage lockers labeled, "ELEPHANT TRANQUILIZER GUN".

When he finally arrived at the Kannon house, the area was inundated and full of flashing blue and red lights from the police cars and ambulances.

The police cruiser that Oscar had stolen was still parked there, and was left on the side of the road, with no sign of Oscar anywhere.

There was a crowd of people gathering on the sidewalk, trying to catch a glimpse of what was going on.

As Marshal Djokeovitch dashed out of his car, he noticed a young rookie police officer stumbling out from the house, and he aimlessly staggered toward a parametric who was at the scene.

"I think, I think, I'm gonna pass out!" he mumbled to the medical attendant, and then he began to violently vomit!

The paramedic quickly broke open a capsule of smelling salts and sat the officer down on a gurney.

The Marshal rushed over to the young officer and inquired what he had seen.

The rookie cop used his sleeve to wipe his mouth and then buried his face into his hands and began to weep.

"It was a horrific freak show in there! The woman was chopped to pieces! Hacked off, grotesque body parts were scattered everywhere!! Her guts and heart were mutilated and yanked out of her torso!

We were searching for her head, and that's when I noticed that the oven was on. It smelled so good, I thought it was something she was cooking for dinner, like a roast and potatoes!

Honestly I was hungry and thought I could sneak a little bite to eat.

When I bent down and opened the oven door, I looked inside, and there was her gorey head, roasting in the oven!!

It was steaming, and her bloody hair and half baked face and crazed eyes were staring right at me from inside of the oven! I freaked out and fell over backwards, and then I stumbled outside!" the young officer cried.

The Marshal then noticed Mr. Kannon, dazed and sitting sideways with the door open in a police cruiser.

He was giving a statement to a detective when Marshal Djokevitch noticed that Rebecca was nowhere to be found.

He immediately rushed over to Mr. Kannon and inquired about his daughter.

"Mr. Kannon, my name is US Marshal Dwain Djokovitch. I'm a friend of Rebecca's from the courthouse. Where is your daughter, I am concerned

that she is targeted and we need to get her in protective custody immediately!" the Marshal stated.

Mr. Kannon, bewildered over the atrocity and the gruesome murder of his wife, was still incognizant.

"Rebecca? Oh, she doesn't live here with us anymore. She moved out and lives with her boyfriend, Charlie. He says they are going to get married, but I always said;

"Why would he buy the cow when he gets the milk for free," Mr. Kannon dubiously stated.

The Marshal was becoming impatient as Mr. Kannon was not realizing the dangerous situation Rebecca was in!

"Where does she live now!" Marshal Djokovich shouted in haste.

Mr. Kannon paused a moment and thought out loud;

"She lives down the street, I'm not sure of the address but it's a white 2 family house. They live on the upstairs floor, I think."

"What's Charlie's surname!!" The Marshal urgently barked.

"Hmmm, his last name…. Charlie, uhmm, Charlie Daniels…oh no that's not it, that's the musician. Oh I know it's Charles Rama! That's it!" exclaimed her father.

The Marshal then darted away and raced over to his car and took hold of the radio microphone, and called in to dispatch.

"This is US Marshal Dwain Djokevitch. I urgently need the address of a Charles Rama, in Aurora! 10-4"

There was a seemingly long pause and then suddenly the dispatcher responded;

"Charles Anthony Rama…#645 Cedar St. Aurora 10-4"

The Marshal instantly started his car and sped off down the street towards Charlie's house. Praying to God that he was not too late.

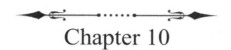

Chapter 10

It was eerily dark and quiet outside of Charlie's house, except for a distant dog's continuous barking.

The first floor apartment was vacant and had a "For Lease" sign taped to the window.

The Marshal parked in the street and noticed that their driveway went alongside the house and curved around back.

He could vaguely see the rear end of Charlie's car parked back there.

The Marshal then noticed that the door leading to the staircase up to the second floor apartment was ajar.

He reached for his microphone and called in for back up and repeated to the dispatch that;

"The perpetrator, Oscar Demento is disguised as a Denver police officer and is armed and extremely dangerous!" and he quickly exited the car.

He removed the long tranquilizer rifle case from the back seat and opened it.

There were several empty elephant darts strapped onto the inside wall of the case, along with extra CO_2 gas cartridges which powered the gun.

The Marshal quickly filled two darts with the Metoprolol, and then screwed a fresh gas cartridge into the rifle.

He opened up the chamber and carefully slid one of the massive tranquilizer darts into the gun and closed the breech.

The Marshal quickly scurried to the back of the house, hoping that there was a back door, when he noticed the abundance of broken glass on the ground, and found Charlie, bloody and beaten and flat out unconscious on top of his car's crushed roof.

He instantly heard banging and pounding and clamoring about, coming from the broken window of the upstairs apartment!

There was someone up there hideously moaning and groaning like a wild beast, and he recognized Oscar's voice as he spoke to himself and his alter ego, the Joker!

It was definitely Oscar, and he was still in there with Rebecca!

The Marshal quickly ran to the front door and raced up the stairs, and burst into the apartment.

He could hear Oscar in the other room talking to himself and grunting hideous ape-like sounds, and he was obviously in a deep psychopathic crazed state of mind.

The bedroom door was wide open when the Marshal crept in and saw Oscar drenched in blood and naked, squatting down firmly on top of Rebecca's naked buttocks while grasping a fist full of her long blonde hair in one hand, and he clenched his massive razor sharp hunting knife in the other.

She was unconscious as Oscar pulled her hair and drew the back of her head towards him.

Lifting her shoulders and breasts off the bed, and arching the nape of her back as he stretched her head

and neck back to him and completely exposed her young feminine throat!

He began to raise his glistening hunting knife and was salivating, as he prepared to slit her throat and carve her beautiful head completely off!

The room was dark, except for a dim night light.

The Marshal was anxious and unsteady, he knew he only had one chance to make the shot, and so he quickly raised the tranquilizer gun, took aim and pulled the trigger!

The gun made a dull pop sound as the dart shot out, however it swerved out of control and it was a clear miss, and stuck directly into the oak headboard, missing Oscar completely!

Oscar instantly turned back and maniacally gazed at the Marshal after he heard the dart gun blast, and hideously smiled at him as he began to reach across her throat with his hunting knife!

The Marshal quickly reloaded the rifle and moved in closer, and then fired the second dart and it stuck deeply into Oscar's neck, and the drug injected directly into Oscar's jugular vein!

The Metoprolol instantly entered his system and Oscar was stunned as he instantly dropped his knife and grabbed the dart from his neck!

The dart had emptied its entire contents and the drug was already in his system, and the adrenalin blocker was acting quickly!

His face was full of rage, and he picked up his knife and turned his attention back towards the Marshal, and screamed a bone chilling shriek as he attempted to leap off the bed at him!

However, it was too late for Oscar, and he was quickly becoming incapasitated.

The knife's handle was soaked with blood, and it slipped out of Oscar's hand as he stumbled and fell off the bed, as if he was having a physical breakdown.

Then he suddenly began to shake uncontrollably and he went into a jaw breaking convulsion as he had just virtually lost all his strength.

The Marshal quickly grabbed Oscar by his long red hair and began punching him furiously in the face, over and over until Oscar's face was mangled and bloodied, and he collapsed onto the floor.

"I always wanted to get you alone, you psycho piece of shit!" the Marshal shouted.

He then removed his 45 caliber revolver and aimed it directly at Oscar's forehead.

"There is no place for you in this world, Demento!" and he began to squeeze the trigger of his massive gun.

Suddenly a policeman came charging into the dimly lit bedroom and saw that there was a man who was dressed as a police officer aiming a gun directly at someone who was incapasitated on the floor!

Instantly the officer shouted;

"Oscar, drop your weapon!" not realizing that it was the Marshal and actually one of them.

When the Marshal moved to reveal his badge, the police officer instinctively pulled his trigger and shot Marshal Djokovitch directly through his heart, and the gunshot was lethal!

The Marshal was dazed and confused as he collapsed to the floor and was dying.

He was still clutching onto his badge and was desperately trying to aim his wavering gun at Oscar's head, as he struggled to pull his trigger and kill Oscar with his last breath of life.

But unfortunately, the Marshal tragically succumbed to death before he could rid the world of Oscar.

The officer who shot him broke down when he suddenly realized that it was not Oscar that he had shot and killed, but a fellow police officer, and it was in fact Oscar that was on the floor unconscious.

More police officers quickly piled in and restrained Oscar with shackles and a straight jacket, as a group of paramedics tried desperately to resuscitate Rebecca and the Marshal.

Rebecca was placed on a gurney, while another group of paramedics removed the Marshal's dead body and a third group tended to Charlie, out in the driveway.

Within minutes both ambulances raced off, and although Marshal Djokovitch was dead, through his courageous actions, he had hopefully saved Rebecca's life.

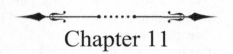

Chapter 11

The two ambulances raced in unison towards Denver's highly regarded hospital, The Level 1 Trauma center.

One ambulance was carrying Charlie and the other, Rebecca.

Both were barely clinging on for their lives.

Charlie was bleeding heavily from his multiple stab and gaping cleaver wounds, and his back was broken and lacerated by broken glass from his fall.

However, being catapulted out of their bedroom window possibly saved Charlie's life, as it put some distance between him and Oscar.

Rebecca was in much dire condition and suffering from multitudes of blunt trauma, and her brain was swelling and hemorrhaging.

Her petite body was severely beaten and brutalized, as she had incurred massive hematomas, lacerations and a tremendous amount of internal trauma and bleeding from her reproductive organs, which were pulverized by Oscar's violent assault on her.

She briefly opened her eyes in the ambulance and strained to utter one word;

"Charlie" and then she lost consciousness once again.

Two of the city's elite trauma teams were standing by and prepared for their immediate arrival.

The ambulances raced into the trauma center's main gate, and instantly stopped at the emergency room doors.

The paramedics who were sitting inside the ambulances and were tending to them, instantly burst out of their compartments and without any hesitation they systematically removed the gurneys and dropped the wheels.

That's when the trauma team took over.

Time was of the essence as they rushed Charlie and Rebecca into the hospital, and they were transported directly into the operating rooms.

The surgeons worked diligently on them for several hours, and it was tedious and delicate work repairing their obliterated bodies.

Charlie had a total of thirteen fractured bones in his back and he received 347 stitches.

He looked as if he had gone through a woodchipper with deep gaping cuts and multitudes of lacerations and splinters from the broken glass shards.

Rebecca was never cut, however she had scores of external contusions and scratches, and her genitalia was decimated and required total cosmetic reconstruction.

Her skull was shattered and she had incurred a massive spider web fracture to her forehead, along with a severe hemorrhaging contusion from the powerful thrusting she received as her forehead pounded against the beds headboard, during Oscar's vicious sexual assault, and now her brain was swelling and bleeding in multiple locations.

Tragically, it caused her to slip into a seriously deep coma.

Several hours later, when the first team brought Charlie out of the operating room, they were physically and emotionally drained.

Not one of them, including the surgeons, had ever seen anyone in such a mangled and butchered state.

Both trauma teams had worked diligently to save the couple, and it was now in God's hands as they were moved to the hospital's ICU.

When the doctors reported to Rebecca's father and Charlie's parents, they were doubtful that the pair would make it through the night, and stated that they might consider;

"Getting things in order and making funeral arrangements."

Mr. Kannon never gave up and together with Charlie's family stayed in the hospital's chapel and prayed for the couple to survive.

Mr. Kannon was torn by the heinous murder of his wife, and the brutal caticlismic rape that his pure and virtuous daughter had just endured, and the grim condition Charlie was in, who fought to protect her.

How could such a horrible thing happen in Littleton?

It was just incomprehensible.

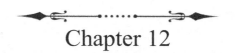

Chapter 12

The police officer who shot and killed Marshal Djokovitch was extremely distraught and was sitting outside on the front steps of the house, with his hands clenched to his scalp.

The body bag containing the Marshal's body was carried past him, and he was dazed and in a state of shock.

There was another officer standing over him, who was trying to console him from his egregious error.

"All I knew was that I heard the 'All Points Bulletin' from on the radio, stating that Oscar was dressed and disguised as a police officer, and when I rushed into the bedroom and saw all the carnage there, and then there was a man dressed as a police officer aiming a gun at who I thought was her boyfriend on the floor! It didn't make sense to me that a US Marshal would be at the scene! I thought it was Demento and he was ready to shoot the boyfriend, so I shot him first!" and then the officer broke down and began to weep.

They secured Oscar, who was bloody and naked and still under the influence of the Metoprolol, by placing a straight jacket on him, then they handcuffed his hands with shackles around his back, and then hog tied his legs back to his hand cuffs.

They wrapped several shackling chains tightly around his body for an added measure of restraint, but

no one was really confident it would hold him once the drug had worn off.

An officer read him his Miranda rights, and then they placed a spit shield over his face as they carried him out like a loaf of bread, and loaded him into an armored prisoner transport vehicle.

Their intention was to quickly transport him back to the ADMAX maximum security prison, which they believed was the only facility possible that could secure and contain him, and hopefully they would get there before the drug would wear off.

Otherwise, he could possibly break free of his restraints and break out of the transport vehicle and escape.

Oscar was shouting obscenities and screaming like a banshee that he didn't do anything wrong and that he was only cleansing the world of all the sluts, until they closed and locked the door on the armored transport vehicle.

When he realized that there was no one there to hear him anymore, he stopped.

The crime scene investigators then took over and combed through the house.

They confiscated Oscar's bloody butcher's cleaver and hunting knife, and took hundreds of photographs.

There was no way Oscar was going to beat this wrap on a technicality. Needless to say, the city slept peacefully with the news that Oscar had struck again, but was captured and returned to prison.

They also recovered the tranquilizer rifle along with the darts and Metoprolol that was used to neutralize Oscar.

They were now well aware of how to control Oscar's explosive and powerful behavior and the prison requisitioned a tranquilizer pistol and a hefty supply of Metoprolol, to keep Oscar in check if necessary.

When Oscar arrived back at the ADMAX prison, he was quickly removed from the prisoner transport vehicle by a cluster of armed guards, and for their safety, he was kept shackled and strapped down onto a rolling gurney.

They escorted him to his maximum security cell, which included a combination toilet-sink and shower. There was no reason to ever let Oscar out of his cell.

Not even for a shower.

His 7'x12' concrete cell had no windows other than the vertical 4"x24" strip of bulletproof plexiglass that was built into the 2" thick solid steel cell door.

In the middle of the door, there was also a narrow 4"x18" horizontal slot, which had its own separate operating door and lock, that would allow a food tray or books to be passed through without opening the larger cell door.

He was quickly rolled into the maximum security ward, still surrounded by the dozen armed guards, and still strapped down and shackled to his gurney.

Incredibly, some of the chain links were beginning to stretch and break open, due to Oscars constant stress on his restraints.

They barely got him into his cell when the Metoprolol had finally worn completely off, and he managed to break free just as the cell door slammed shut!

He was wild with rage as he managed to tear off his straight jacket and then he quickly snapped the shackles and chains off of himself.

He immediately turned his attention to the gurney which they blatantly left behind and he began smashing it against the cell door, trying to break out!

However, the guards were not concerned at all, since once the cell door was locked, they were confident that even a bull elephant couldn't break out of there.

The Warden had also installed an experimental "knockout" nerve gas system into Oscar's cell, which was designed to incapacitate violent or unruly inmates, so that in the event these prisoners were not cooperating or were being disruptive in their cells, they could be easily subdued without the need of physically opening up their doors and jeopardizing the safety of the guards.

"Let's give Oscar a good night's rest," one of the guards jokingly stated, and he pushed the red button which was located outside his cell door.

The room was instantly flooded with a giant pulse of fog, and within seconds Oscar was unconscious and flat out on the floor.

A few guards rushed in wearing gas masks and rubber gloves, and immediately confiscated the obliterated gurney and they removed the remaining shackles and chains from his sweaty and blood splattered body.

They left Oscar lying there on the floor, and tossed a prison uniform on top of him to wear, and then they quickly left the cell and slammed the steel door shut!

The guards then switched on an exhaust fan and the room quickly cleared and Oscar soon began to stir and moan, as he slowly regained consciousness.

He was baffled about what had just transpired and how quickly the gas took effect.

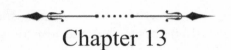

Chapter 13

In the following week, Oscar was arraigned and no bail was set due to the heinous and violent nature of Oscar's crimes.

The cities prosecution team was well prepared this time and brought up a long list of capital punishment charges beginning with, First degree murder, Impersonating a police officer, Theft of a police vehicle, Assault with a deadly weapon, Intent to commit murder, Assault, Rape, Malice and much more.

Oscar's court appointed attorney immediately filed for an insanity plea bargain, however the prosecution wouldn't have any of that.

The prosecution had in their possession the document that positively stated that the Psychotherapy Checklist test (or PCL) had already been given to Oscar at his previous court hearing, and he was cleared of having any psychopathic disorders.

According to those results, the prosecution argued, Oscar was found to be a noble citizen with not even a remote trace of psychopathic tendencies.

Unfortunately for Oscar, his PCL stunt backfired on him the second time around, and nixed his chances of avoiding the death penalty, since it unequivocally proved that he was not insane or a psychopath.

His only defensive position now was that, Officer Laredo, who was in cahoots with his Uncle Ned tried

to gas him to death while he was locked in the back seat of the police cruiser.

He claimed that it was an act of self-defense, and it was instigated by Police officer Laredo and his Uncle Ned which indeed initiated his killing spree.

Oscar's defense attorney claimed that if the incident in which they attempted to kill Oscar as he was trapped in the backseat of the police cruiser had never occurred, Uncle Ned and everyone else for that matter, would still be alive today.

The jury did not buy Oscar's rendition of the story, as there were no witnesses to corroborate that Officer Laredo and Uncle Ned were in "cahoots" although there was some evidence of a hose laying around on the driveway with traces of carbon monoxide, and an envelope full of money found at the Demento house.

It seemed that the officer might have attempted to gas Oscar.

But Oscar took much pleasure decimating the two men rather than just running away for help, and that didn't sit well with the jury.

There was not the carnival atmosphere at this trial as there was at his last hearing.

There were no television cameras allowed in the courtroom and besides several tabloid reporters, and a few local news teams, it seemed that everyone knew that it was going to be a quick trial and most people lost interest in it, and Oscar.

During the trial though, to keep Oscar from enraging himself and breaking free of his restraints, he was kept under control with dozens of injections of Metoprolol administered by a court appointed nurse.

The trial only lasted three days, and in the end, the jury found Oscar "Guilty" for the assault and battery on Charlie and the horrific assault and rape of Rebecca.

And "Guilty" for the murder of Mrs. Kannon, and his Uncle Ned, however in respect to the murder of police Officer Laredo, he was found innocent by reason of self defence, with the exception that the dismemberment aspect of that murder was unjustified and heinous.

And so Oscar was sentenced to death for the murder of his Uncle Ned and Mrs. Kannon, and his attempted murder assault on Charlie and Rebecca.

It didn't really matter at that point, convicting him of dismemberment and malice for his assault on Officer Laredo.

He was going to death row anyways without any possibility of parole.

The jury was unanimous and his sleazy defense attorney immediately filed his countless years of appeals.

Oscar wasn't going to go away so fast.

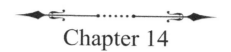

Chapter 14

The morning Colorado sun rose over the trauma center, however things inside the ICU were not so sunny.

Charlie was being kept sedated and on a ventilator.

His heart stopped twice throughout the night but they were miraculously able to restart it both times, and by morning he was slightly more stable.

Rebecca was slowly stabilizing, however she was in a deep coma due to her severe brain injuries.

The doctors reconstructed her, but sadly they feared that even if she did survive, and if she came out of this horrific and barbaric assault without permanent brain damage, she might never be the same again or lead a normal life.

As the days passed Charlie's vitals became stronger and they removed his breathing tube.

They stopped the induced sedation and his parents waited by his bedside praying for him to wake up.

No one could ever imagine the horrific event which had taken place at their upstairs apartment, and;

"Why them?"

They were both decent, honest, church going citizens, with their whole lives and future in front of them.

Now this diabolical smudge has wiped out their inner beings, and neither of them was ever going to be the same again.

They both will carry the enormous weight of this unforgettable and tragic night.

Charlie will alway feel the guilt of not being able to protect his soul mate and bare the scars of the assault.

Rebecca will tragically have a constant reminder of that sweet and bitter night, making love with Charlie and then minutes later to be violently raped and assaulted by a mad psychopathic maniac.

If she survives, how could she ever make love again, and mask out that horrific night, and ever recount her feelings that she once had with Charlie.

Nothing will ever be the same again between the two of them, and it was neither one's fault.

Only time will tell if they can survive and then pull through this tragedy.

Several hours had passed and it seemed that Charlie was coming around.

He slowly opened his black eyes and they were full of blood.

He struggled to speak, but his very first words were strained;

"Is... Rebecca, okay?"

His parents were overjoyed that their son was alive and seemingly out of the woods. He was still very weak, and it would be another week or so before they could begin removing the countless stitches and staples that held his body together.

There were still dozens of minute shards of glass that were still embedded deeply into his body, and dozens of pins holding his fractured and damaged bones together, but he was healing.

He was constantly asking about Rebecca, never once giving thought to his own condition and well being.

However, they were cautious about what Charlie needed to know.

They told him that after he was thrown out of the 2nd story window, Oscar turned his attention towards Rebecca and she was attacked by the devil himself.

However, neither they nor the doctors divulged that she was horrifically raped and her reproductive organs and genitalia were obliterated by the beast.

All he was told was that Oscar had beaten her very badly, but thanks to the US Marshal who showed up literally in the nick of time, he saved her life.

When Charlie was finally strong enough, he asked to see Rebecca.

They told him that she was in the next room, but her head was seriously hurt and she was in a deep coma.

However, she was alive and that gave him hope.

As he layed in his hospital bed and healed, he dreamt of the days to come that he and Rebecca could be back together again, and finally be married and start a family.

He reminisced of their pillow talk about what it was going to be like once they were married.

The grand wedding, loving each other forever, and starting a family. They both loved children and hoped for a very large family to fill their house with love and joy.

Now unbeknown to Charlie, that dream was now most unlikely if not impossible.

And so was the happy life they had so often spoken about and planned together.

Thanks to that maniacal beast, their future was ruined.

Blindsided on the most glorious and romantic evening of their lives.

As fate would have it, she was at the wrong place at the wrong time. And this horrific event was a powerful steam train heading her way from the very first moment, when she decided that she wanted to become a court stenographer.

After a few more days of resting in bed, and with help from the nurses, Charlie was allowed to get out of his bed and use the bathroom.

His back was stiff and his muscles ached, and he felt the stinging pain of the glass shards which were still lost in his body.

He hobbled along his path to the bathroom, resembling Frankenstein as he was covered with massive contusions and was plastered with bandages and grotesquely exposed stitches and staples all over his body.

It hurt to walk that short distance, but as time went on he was getting stronger, and one day when he noticed that no one was watching him, he went directly out the door to find Rebecca.

He rounded the corner out his doorway and immediately heard the soft voice of Rebecca's father in her hospital room.

He was sitting beside her, holding her limp hand and was in deep prayer as he wept.

Charlie managed to peek in and was shocked and horrified to see her in the condition she was in.

She appeared to be badly beaten and unconscious, and she was surrounded by all sorts of hospital machinery.

Her head and face was completely wrapped with thick gauze and tape, and spots of blood were bleeding through the bandages.

Her mouth and nose were filled with all sorts of tubes, and several liquid bags of medicines hung from a stand as the drugs dripped down through narrow plastic tubes, which were injected intravenously into a junction mechanism taped down on her inner forearm.

Charlie began to tear up and he started to take a step toward her when a nurse stopped him and escorted him back to his bed.

The last joyful thing Charlie remembered from that night was how happy they both were and how beautiful she was as they embraced as true soulmates, after finally consummating their love for each other.

Now she was somewhere else and nothing ever will be the same again.

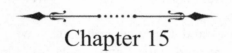

Chapter 15

Several weeks had passed and Charlie was well enough to be released from the hospital.

However, sadly Rebecca was still unconscious and in a deep coma.

Once Charlie was strong enough he was allowed to sit and visit with her every day.

The journey to recovery was long and hard for Charlie.

Countless hours of rehabilitation and physical therapy.

He underwent at least 3 more surgical procedures and some cosmetic plastic surgery to fix some of the horrendous gaping scars left by Oscar's brutal attack.

It was uncomfortable for him to return to their home, in fact he stayed at his parents house and continued his recuperation there for some time. Eventually, he felt that for his own well being, he had to return to their apartment and face his demons, so that he could move forward.

His father drove him to the house and he noticed that the upstairs window was repaired and his car and the broken glass were gone, probably cleaned up by the landlord.

He continued on to the staircase and struggled as he painfully climbed up to the second floor.

The apartment looked tidied up and he noticed the box of dead dehydrated roses with its bright red ribbon still on the kitchen table.

He became upset when he thought about that beautiful night that he expected to have, and the surprise of her engagement ring hidden inside a fortune cookie.

He thought for sure the ring must have been thrown away during the clean up, along with the Chinese take out which he had also left on the kitchen table.

But to his surprise, when he opened the refrigerator, there sat the small condiments bag from the Chinese takeout.

He held his breath as he peeked inside and then he smiled for the first time in weeks.

He reached into the sack and removed the fortune cookie and held it to his heart as he began to cry.

His father put his hand on his shoulder and told him to "be strong".

That special fortune cookie was all Charlie needed, and his father packed some things from Charlie's dresser into a duffle bag and the two men silently left.

Charlie held the fortune cookie in his hand and asked his father if he could take him back to the hospital, so that he could be with Rebecca.

When he arrived, he hoped that Rebecca would somehow be miraculously recovered, and this whole nightmare was just a bad dream. When he quietly entered her room, she was sleeping peacefully.

Almost the same way as that night when he returned home with her engagement ring and flowers.

He carefully sat down on the bed beside her, and just watched her as he prayed to God not to take her from him.

He began to tear up as he cracked open the stale fortune cookie which contained her engagement ring, and he deeply gazed into the sparkling faceted crystal as he held it between his fingers.

He couldn't hold back his tears any longer and he became overwhelmed with sadness and he cried.

"Rebecca... I love you so much, will you marry me?" Charlie managed to choke out through his tears.

He then lifted her hand and gently slid the ring onto her ring finger.

It fit perfectly.

He continued to sit there beside her, dreaming and praying as he begged God to revive her, but nothing changed and the machines continued to rhythmically pump and do their jobs.

He leaned over and kissed her bandaged face when he heard Rebecca's father in the hallway, and he was raising his voice at the doctors.

"That's impossible!! how could this be?" he shouted.

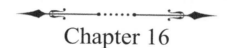

Chapter 16

Charlie couldn't understand what all the arguing was about when he overheard the doctor speaking with Mr. Kannon outside in the hallway.

He thought that they were possibly contemplating ending Rebecca's treatments, and were going to pull the plug and let her die.

He rushed out into the hospital corridor to find out what was going on between the doctor and Rebecca's father.

When Mr. Kannon saw Charlie, he quickly turned away and began punching the wall.

"What's going on??!" exclaimed Charlie.

The doctor stared at him dumbfounded, and didn't say a word.

"Come on man, that's my girlfriend in there! What's going on?!" Charlie insisted.

"Mr. Kannon, do I have your permission to inform Charlie of the situation?" questioned the doctor.

Extremely distressed, he nodded his head "yes", then turned in disgust and rushed towards the hospital's elevator.

Then the doctor quickly turned to speak to Charlie.

"I'm sorry Charlie, but even though Rebecca is your girlfriend, you are not her next of kin, and her father is calling all the shots regarding Rebecca's healthcare. The hospital rules are pretty strict about

giving out information and following protocol. Now that her father gave us permission to speak to you, we have some disturbing news to tell you," stated the doctor.

Charlie became confused and frightened, he thought that Rebecca's prognosis was grimm and they were going to stop treating her.

"Please don't turn off the machines! I'll do whatever it takes to pay for her medical bills, no matter how long it takes! Just please, give her more time," Charlie cried.

The doctor put his hand on Charlie's shoulder and spoke to him;

"Charlie, we all know how much you love Rebecca, and that you would do anything for her. This is not about shutting off the machines and giving up on her. It's something different and everyone is going to have to be really strong right now. As you could see, Mr. Kannon is taking it pretty hard and that's not going to help matters. There are going to be some big decisions to be made, and it's all going to fall on Rebecca's father, unfortunately you have no say in the matter since Rebecca is not your wife," stated the doctor.

Charlie was just a simple man and was confused by the doctor's rhetoric.

"Can you just please just tell me what's going on, you are scaring the hell out of me!" Charlie exclaimed.

The doctor looked dismally at Charlie and then he began to speak in a serious tone;

"Charlie, we discovered through a hematology test that Rebecca might be pregnant. And when we

performed a pregnancy test on her this morning, it confirmed that she is in fact pregnant."

Charlie became dizzy and his world began to spin out of control as those words drummed into his ears.

The doctor continued;

"Rebecca's father informed me that his daughter confided in her mother and told her that the two of you were not physically involved since she was waiting to get married before having intercourse with you. So our conclusion is that the baby she is carrying is Oscar Demento's offspring, and Mr. Kannon wants us to preform an abortion as soon as possible."

Upon hearing that information Charlie became faint and collapsed onto the floor.

The doctor immediately ordered a nurse to inject a sedative into Charlie's arm, and when he finally awoke, several hours had passed.

He suddenly came to his senses and found himself lying on a cot in Rebecca's room, and she was gone!

Charlie staggered to his feet and started shouting for the doctors and Rebecca.

He feared that they had taken her and were preforming the abortion!

He had to stop them, and they needed to know that it may be in fact his child, and not Oscars in her womb!

A nurse came rushing over from the nurses station to find out why Charlie was so upset.

He grabbed her and asked her if she knew where Rebecca was, and she confirmed his worst nightmare.

She was in the operating room and they were preforming the abortion!

Charlie shook the nurse and grilled her as to where the operating room was, and she haphazardly pointed toward the end of the corridor!

Charlie raced down the hallway as fast as his recovering body could move!

But just as he was ready to barge in, he spotted the doctors pushing the swinging doors outward and they were already wheeling Rebecca out of the recovery room, with her father sadly walking next to her unconscious body.

Charlie broke down and began to cry, as the surgical team and Rebecca's father approached him!

"What have you monsters done! Are you not a Christian minister who is an anti-abortion advocate! Every baby is a precious life, is what you preached to your congregation, you son of a bitch!! Rebecca and I consummated our love minutes before that pervert invaded our home! That baby you murdered might have been ours!" Charlie cried out.

There was suddenly a look of horrid shock that overcame Mr. Kannon when he heard that news.

"You consummated your love? What the hell does that mean, Charlie?!" Mr. Kannon shouted.

"It means what it sounds like, and now you murdered my child you hypocritical bastard!!" Charlie shouted back.

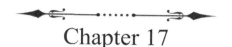

Chapter 17

The doctor intervened and took Charlie aside as Rebecca's entourage continued on, and returned her comatose body back to her room.

Charlie was beside himself with grief, as his posture sunk.

First he lost Rebecca and now his child.

He began to cry uncontrollably and the doctor led him to a private conference room where he told Charlie to take a seat and calm down.

Charlie was beyond upset with the thought that they had just murdered his child, and with her Christian minister fathers permission.

"Charlie, I have good and bad news for you," the doctor stated.

Charlie tried to gain control of his weeping and began to pause for a moment.

The doctor continued;

"Well Charlie, before we do any abortion procedures in this hospital, it's extremely rare when the mother is in the condition Rebecca is in. We would usually go to the husband and get his permission to perform a procedure such as that. But, because as I explained to you earlier, you are not married to Rebecca, her father is her next of kin and her medical conservator. The thought of Rebecca carrying that human waste's baby in her belly sickened your father to the point that he threw away

all his religious beliefs and moral values, and wanted, what he perceived to be, that demon's baby scoured out of his daughter's body."

Charlie blankly stared at the doctor, not feeling any better about the situation.

"You said there was some good news?" Charlie quietly inquired.

"Yes Charlie, there is some more good and bad news, and I want you to be strong when I tell you, because it's not going to be easy."

Charlies straightened his posture and sat upright.

And the doctor continued;

"Charlie, we were required to run a DNA test on Rebecca's amniotic fluid for medical research purposes. Some scientists want to study how and why the DNA shifts from forming a commonly normal innocent fetus, and then at some point it metastasizes and becomes radicalized to the point where it mutates and causes the fetus to develop into a psychopathic individual.

When we took Rebecca's samples to the lab, they were thoroughly analyzed and there was an anomaly. The samples were found to contain three different sources of DNA. One was from Rebecca, but then there were the two others which were completely different from each other. To state it in layman's terms we know that one bracket of the unknown DNA was from Oscar Dimento based on the overwhelming quantity of semen we recovered from inside of her, but the other bracket, we were totally confused about, since Mr. Kannon stated that you and Rebecca were remaining celibut. But now, since you recently

revealed that the two of you copulated prior to the assault, it makes more sense now," the doctor stated.

Charlie just sat there confused and not really understanding what the hell the doctor was saying.

"I'm not really following you, Doc," Charlie nervously stated.

The physician was getting frustrated and stared deeply into Charlie's eyes.

"Charlie, we did not perform the abortion on Rebecca, because there was a positive conclusion that there was another man who was the father of one of the babies, and now it seems to make sense that that man is you, Charlie," the doctor stated.

Charlie's head was spinning out of control, as it was now a fact that Rebecca was actually pregnant with his child.

Charlie became elated and it brought new life and hope into his soul.

"You said there was bad news, too?" Charlie half heartedly questioned.

"Yes Charlie, there is some very bad news. Maybe you didn't catch what I said. I stated that you are the father of one of the babies. The bad news is that we did an ultrasound to see what was going on inside her. We have verified proof that Rebecca is carrying twins. One of them is yours, and the other baby is Oscars!

It's rare but possible, and there have been some cases documented where a woman was impregnated by two different men at the same time. It's a phenomenon called Heteropaternal Superfecundation.

These twins are fraternal, which means that they won't be identical since there were two separate eggs

present at the time of conception. Your sperm hit one egg and Oscars hit the other," the doctor explained.

Charlie couldn't believe his ears as he sunk down into his chair and placed his hands over his face in horrific agony.

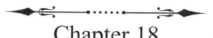

Chapter 18

Oscar's days in the ADMAX high security prison were not complicated or extraordinary.

He knew that he had at least 15-20 years of court appeals before they would actually carry out his execution, and so he lived on death row in a specially designed ward of the prison which housed the nations most notorious and violent criminals.

These cells were uniquely designed since they adjoined a small exterior 400 square ft courtyard, which had dense iron bars covering the top and reinforced with spools of electrified razor wire.

The walls of the courtyard were 50 ft tall and solid concrete.

The courtyard was designed to comply with the state prison board's mandate of an hour of outdoor recreation 5 days per week for all inmates.

It was argued that a prisoner, even the worst, which has lost his or her rights to be included in society, were still deemed certain humanitarian rights of liberty.

Which virtually meant that inmates should be allowed a "given" amount of outdoor time from their cells.

"Time" could be defined as minutes, and as long as they could see a bit of the sky, it was considered "Outdoors".

No one was taking any chances handling these criminals, and so the special annex was designed so that the exercise area was joined and shared with Oscar's and several other inmates' cells, by remote controlled two inch thick solid steel doors.

If the instance arose that Oscar or any other inmate would not comply and return to their cell from the exercise area, the floor of the outdoor area was electrified and they would find out the hard way to obey, and then would comply and do what they were told.

Oscar's meals were served to him on a paper tray, through the 4" slot in his cell door.

It was wide enough so that when opened from the outside a prisoner could place their hands through the opening and be handcuffed.

The prison food wasn't meant to be tasty, it was designed to have a nutritional element to it, and the portions were enough to barely satisfy them.

Even their final meals for the death row inmates were unspectacular.

If an inmate desired lobster or filet mignon for his "last meal" it was certain he would never ever get it.

The prison would most likely accommodate their request to whatever was available in the kitchen at the time, since gourmet food such as lobster and prime beef would never be on the prison's menu, even for a death row criminal's final meal.

Lobster would be substituted with a piece of fish and the Filet mignon most likely with a salisbury steak or a hamburger.

Often when Oscar's food arrived, he wouldn't think twice about tossing his meals against the wall of

his cell, but other times he sat graciously as if he were fine dining at a 5 star restaurant at his desk, and he ate quietly.

You never knew what to expect from Oscar, except the worst.

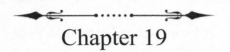

Chapter 19

The news about Rebecca's pregnancy was bittersweet for Charlie.

On one hand he was blessed with a child, and it was a gift from Rebecca despite her unconscious condition.

On the other hand he was abhorred that she was also carrying Oscar's baby, and that monster was living inside of her and sharing her womb with his child.

He feared the worst in that at some point, Oscar's spawn could hurt or kill his baby, and he began to panic!

"Doctor, please you have to get that maniac's baby out of her! It will undoubtedly kill my child once it's strong enough! Get back in that operating room and abort that demon's seed!" Charlie shouted.

The doctor looked down at the floor and was surprised to hear those words coming from Charlie.

"What happened to the sanctity of life, Charlie? A few minutes ago you were pro life, you said abortion was murder, and now all of the sudden when it effects you, there goes all the morals and religion.

To be honest with you son, it would be impossible to only abort one of the fetuses. And so, unless you want to kill your own child in the process, that won't be an option. I can tell you that both babies are female, and just because Oscar is a psychopathic

murderer, it doesn't necessarily mean his child will be one too. Not to mention that even though it is Oscar's baby it's still Rebecca's baby too.

Furthermore, there is a tremendous risk that Rebecca might not ever awake from her coma, or she could die from the stress of gestation, especially with twins who will tax her body heavily.

She could even die before the babies are developed enough, Charlie," the doctor firmly stated.

Charlie placed his hands over his face and rubbed his eyes in distress.

What a predicament they were in.

Rebecca became pregnant after being abstinent all her life, and only after they made true love for the very first time.

God blessed them and made a baby from their love of one another.

Then somehow Satan reared his ugly head and she was horrifically raped and impregnated with that psychopath Oscar's sinister seed, which is now living inside her, and she is procreating it.

"How can this be happening!" he thought.

Suddenly Charlie noticed that a nurse came running out from Rebecca's room and approached the doctor and Charlie.

"She opened her eyes!" the nurse shouted in delight.

The doctor and Charlie rushed down the hallway and into Rebecca's room.

She was surrounded by a team of nurses that were all gazing down at her.

When Charlie and the doctor made their way next to her bed, they found her drearily laying there, barely

awake with her eyes slightly open! Charlie was instantly elated, in that he could just barely see her deep blue eyes, which were slightly peeking through her heavy eyelids.

The doctor quickly removed her oxygen mask and checked her vital stats.

Her brain signals and motor neurons were rapidly recovering and she was beginning to move her fingers.

She had been unconscious for approximately eight weeks and her muscles had begun to atrophy.

She was by far no way out of the woods, but it was very promising that she was awake from her coma and fidgeting.

Charlie instantly took her hand and he told her that he loved her, but there was no response.

Just a dead stare at the ceiling.

Then she began to tear up and she visibly began struggling to utter two words;

"Love...Charlie"

"I'm here Rebecca!" Charlie jubilantly stated and he took her hand in his.

The doctor quickly ordered everyone to leave the room, and told one of the nurses to call Rebecca's father.

He stated to everyone that she could drift in and out of her coma, especially if she was over-stimulated, and so she needed peace and quiet.

Charlie wanted to sit and stay with her, but he was escorted out of the room by one of the exiting nurses, as they were cheerfully chattering amongst each other.

It was a miracle and Charlie was feeling optimistic!

But no one really knew the extent of Rebecca's injuries.

Even though she was coming out of her coma, there still was the issue of brain damage and to what extent Rebecca could regain her functions and return to normal, if such a thing was possible.

Charlie sat in the family lounge contemplating all of the news.

If Rebecca does fully awake from her coma, how is she going to be? Will she still have her senses? Will she still love him? How will she feel about being pregnant with both of their babies?

These were the difficult questions that Charlie was contemplating, but no one will know the answers for sure until Rebecca is up and ready.

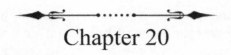

Chapter 20

Upon receiving the news of Rebecca's condition, Mr. Kannon quickly left the church pulpit and raced back to the hospital.

When he entered Rebecca's room he was surprised to see Charlie sitting beside her and holding her hand, and that she was still unconscious.

He sadly presumed that her awakening was a false positive when she opened her eyes and she seemed to come out of her coma for the moment.

Charlie saw his hopeless and distressed expression after he anxiously came into her room, expecting to find his only child awake.

"She's just sleeping, Mr. Kannon. She is not in a coma," Charlie softly stated.

He let out a great sigh of relief, and sat down next to Charlie.

"The doctor put her on a light sedative to sleep. He said that sleeping will help heal her brain and it's different from her being in a coma. She was really groggy the first time I saw her with her eyes open, but she drifts in and out," Charlie whispered.

"What are we going to do about that psycho bastard's baby she's carrying?" Mr. Kannon whispered to Charlie.

"The doctor said that it's her choice what to do after the baby is born. No one knows God's path, or that the baby will even be evil like her deranged

father. There is no way to preform an abortion with out harming the other baby, my daughter," Charlie affirmed.

Her father just sat there with a dire look of anguish, which was heavily painted on his face.

"There must be something we can do, that baby will be a constant reminder of that horrific attack she went through, and how can she love a baby that was a product of that?!" Mr. Kannon harshly stated.

"First we have to take care of Rebecca and get her well.

We need to pray that she will be able to come out of this trauma and be okay. We still don't know the extent of her physical condition and how much brain damage she incurred. The doctor said it might be months or even years until she is even able to function on her own," Charlie whispered.

Her father lowered his head and replied;

"I'm really scared that she might be a vegetable and never be the same as she once was. I don't think I can take care of her, Charlie. With my ministry work and working at the church, I don't have a lot of money. I can't afford the help she may need," Mr. Kannon softly stated as his eyes filled with tears.

"Don't worry about that, Mr. Kannon, I'll take care of her," Charlie firmly stated.

And he reached down into his coat pocket and revealed the ring box with the engagement ring still inside.

"That night, after we were together, I got up to get this ring from the kitchen where I had left the Chinese takeout food that I brought home that evening. I had the ring hidden in a fortune cookie and I was going to

surprise her with it. My plan was to ask her to marry me that night.

When I got up, that's when I heard a strange noise and that maniac busted into our room!

Weeks later, when I finally had the courage to go back into my house and get some of my belongings, I feared that a police officer or the landlord might have thrown the food bag away with the ring in it, since it was left out the whole time. But when I opened the refrigerator, to my surprise I found the little bag containing the duck sauce, crispy noodles and fortune cookies inside on the shelf.

I thanked God that it wasn't thrown out!

I instantly tore the little bag apart and found the stale fortune cookie and Rebecca's engagement ring still inside. It took me about a year to pay this ring off, and the day of the assault was the day I was finally able to bring it home.

While I sat with Rebecca as she was in her deep coma, I asked her to marry me everyday, and I'm still waiting for her answer."

Mr. Kannon gave Charlie a pat on the shoulder and then smiled with approval that Charlie would hopefully someday become his son in law.

"It's in God's hands now Charlie, God's hands," stated Mr. Kannon and he closed his eyes and they both prayed for Rebecca.

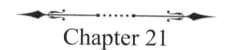

Chapter 21

It wasn't long before one of the hospital staff leaked the news to some of the sleazy tabloid reporters that were sneaking into the hospital, looking for a scoop on the Oscar Demento story.

The latest narrative was now all over the tabloid newspapers, and even on some of the evening television gossip shows.

The headline read;

"KANNON'S LOADED WITH A DUD!!"

And the story read that Rebecca Kannon, was drifting in and out of her coma, and the fact that she was the woman who was violently raped by the notorious Oscar Demento, was now pregnant with twins!

And that one of her babies was Oscar Demento's spawn and the other one was her boyfriend Charlie Rama's baby!

The drama was revived and it was keeping the public on the edge of their seats!

In Las Vegas, bets were ghoulishly being placed at all the casino's, and odds were set to 75/1 that Oscar's offspring would murder its twin in the womb!

It was front page news all over the world, and the nation was glued to the story!

Charlie was inundated with requests to appear on television to tell his story, but he refused.

He was upset with the general public, that to them, this was some big entertainment show, and he and Rebecca were under the microscope for their enjoyment.

They didn't care one bit about them or their feelings, or if their baby was in danger.

The fact that people were placing bets that Oscar's baby was going to kill his unborn daughter in the womb was extremely disturbing to Charlie.

Fortunately, Oscar had no idea what was going on.

He was sequestered in his cell with no television or newspapers. Occasionally books were handed out to the inmates, but the prison staff made it a point to keep Oscar in the dark about all current events, especially anything related to Charlie and Rebecca.

Had Oscar ever found out that he had a child out there, it could cause him to erupt and try to escape.

Even though it was impossible for anyone to break out of the ADMAX facility, no one was taking any chances with Oscar and his enlarged Hypothalamus and Adrenal glands.

There were still six months left on Rebecca's gestation period, and Charlie couldn't help but to contemplate when he was going to tell Rebecca about the babies, and how she was going to handle it.

He hoped that she would do the right thing and offer to give up Oscar's baby for adoption, but the problem was, who in their right mind would ever want to adopt Oscar's baby, a probable psychopathic demon?

Or what if Rebecca chose to keep Oscar's baby, and that wicked witch would live with them and their daughter!

These kinds of depressing thoughts were driving Charlie into a frenzy.

But first, Rebecca had to recover from her injuries, and then there was going to be plenty of time to figure things out later.

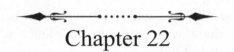

Chapter 22

Despite Rebecca momentarily peeking her eyes open, she was still in a catatonic state and the doctors were beginning to get anxious that maybe her brain damage was more extensive, and Rebecca might not ever be the same again.

Charlie continued to sit beside her and hold her hand, praying for her to come back to him.

He slept there in a chair next to her, sometimes all night long.

Even Charlie was beginning to lose hope, until one evening he sat next to her bed and tenderly held her hand.

He was tired and he rested his forehead on a pillow which was next to her, and he closed his eyes.

He thought he was dreaming when he felt Rebecca's grip tighten and she squeezed his hand.

And then he couldn't believe his ears when he heard the faint words;

"Yes, Charlie. I will marry you."

It was Rebecca's soft feminine voice and he lifted his head in jubilation and saw her bright blue eyes gleaming and her wonderful strained smile on her face!

It wasn't a dream!

Charlie broke down and began to cry.

God had answered his prayers and returned his love back to him!

He carefully wrapped his arms around her frail body and held her tightly.

"I thought I lost you, Rebecca! Now I'm never going to let go of you!" Charlie cried.

She was barely able to lift her atrophied arms, but managed to awkwardly embrace Charlie.

A nurse who was walking by her room noticed that she was miraculously awake and moving, and so she quickly entered the room. She anxiously took some vital signs and then rushed to the nurses station to contact the doctor and Rebecca's father.

She was very weak and it was difficult for her to move, considering that she was in bed and in and out of a coma for the past 3 months.

The doctors quickly arrived and ordered everyone out of the room while they did a mental exam on her.

Her father arrived there shortly after, and was disappointed that he was also kept out of her room, while they continued their exam.

When the doctors finally exited her room, they reported that she was dazed and confused.

She didn't know why she was in the hospital or the events that landed her in here.

And all she can say is;

"Yes, I want to marry you, Charlie!"

We don't know the extent of the brain damage, but it's promising that she can even speak a few words.

It might take some time before we know for sure, but we should know soon enough. We are going to start tomorrow with her physical and mental therapy sessions," stated the doctor.

Charlie was confused by the doctor's medical prognosis and asked what it all ment.

The doctor responded;

"Simply stated, she has amnesia, Charlie. She doesn't remember being raped or the violent attack. It might be a blessing in disguise that she can't remember that horrific event, but she seems to remember you and somehow while she was deep in her coma, she heard you ask for her hand in marriage. Her memory could be jarred at any moment and she could remember what happened. But most often the tragic event is so deeply suppressed that it never comes back. You and her father are going to face some tough choices. When are you going to tell her that she is pregnant?" The doctor questioned.

The two men looked at each other and shrugged their shoulders.

"I think we should wait until she gets stronger and more together before we drop that bomb," stated Rebecca's father.

The doctor nodded in agreement and left the conversation.

Charlie and her father then entered the room where Rebecca was quietly lying and she was slightly smiling at them.

Her father rushed in and carefully hugged her and cried, when he suddenly realized that she didn't know that her mother was dead.

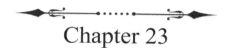

Chapter 23

In the following days, Rebecca was showing signs of improvement.

Although she was still bed ridden and tired, she was becoming more alert, but still sleeping most of the day.

The nurses told Charlie not to worry;

"It is the way the brain heals itself."

A physical therapist came to her room and started to do simple things with Rebecca.

It seemed that due to the extent of her brain injury, and the depth and length of her coma, she had lost her ability to move and speak with coordination.

The mental therapist saw signs that Rebecca still maintained her cognitive senses, and that besides having amnesia and difficulty speaking she could be fine with a lot more therapy.

You could see it in her eyes that Rebecca had questions, but was unable to put sentences together.

How did she get there? Who did this to her?

And then finally, when Charlie arrived at her room later that morning with a fresh bouquet of flowers, she uttered these words;

"My... moth-er?"

Charlie sadly sat down next to her on her bed and contemplated what to say.

He took a deep breath and built up his courage, and took the initiative as he held her hand and she stared into his eyes.

"I guess you are wondering how you got here and why you haven't seen your mother yet," Charlie sadly stated.

Rebecca's eyes opened wide and she wanted to know what happened.

Charlie continued;

"A very bad person, a maniac, showed up at your parents house when your mom was home alone. Apparently he saw you at the courthouse, and he was looking for you.

He forced his way inside and I'm sorry to say, he murdered your sweet innocent mother," and Charlie paused.

Rebecca turned away and buried her face into her pillow to conceal her grief, and felt that it was her fault, and that she was the cause of her mothers death.

She cried as Charlie caressed her back, and he felt it was better to continue and get it all out on the table at once, rather than just slowly pull the bandage off.

"Somehow he discovered our address at your parents house, and later that night he broke into our apartment looking for you.

I fought him with all my might to protect you, but he cut me up pretty badly with the weapons he brought, and he was so strong that he finally launched me through our bedroom window, and I was knocked unconscious when I landed on top of my car.

Once I was out of his way, he turned his attention toward you, and he attacked you. He was preparing to

kill you, when a US Marshal showed up and shot him with a tranquilizer dart, just in the nick of time."

Charlie lifted his shirt and revealed the massive scars and scar tissue which covered his torso.

Rebecca's eyes continued to tear up and she was visibly upset with the tragic news about her mother and what Charlie had gone through, as he was trying to protect her.

He took her hand and squeezed it as she wiped her tears.

I have something else to tell you Rebecca, but it's going to have to wait.

Charlie then climbed up on the bed and layed down next to her and held her as she continued to weep over the death of her mother.

"The good news is that we still have each other, and I'm going to take care of you," Charlie softly stated as he caressed her soft blond hair.

He reconsidered that maybe he should have held off a little while longer on the news of her mother and the assault. But she needed to know, and rather than keep her in the dark, he told her.

However, it was too soon to mention anything about the rape and the pregnacy, though.

He discussed it with her father and they both decided that it would be better for Rebecca to "not remember" or "be told" about that horrific assault just yet, if ever.

She didn't need to know about that tragic event, and maybe, just maybe she could go on and lead a normal life without that enormous black cloud hanging over her.

As far as the pregnancy, Rebecca's father had already signed papers with a foreign adoption agency, while Rebecca was still in a coma and comatose.

The papers stated that, when Rebecca eventually goes into labor, and Oscar's daughter is born, that baby would be immediately confiscated by agents of a Peruvian adoption agency and transported to an ancient South American monastery, which was hidden away in the desolate mountainous area of Peru.

At the time, no one expected Rebecca to come out of her coma and obviously no one wanted to deal with Oscar's psychopathic baby.

But now that she was awake and out of her coma, that plan might be off the table.

Unless someone could convince her otherwise.

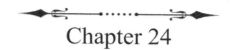

Chapter 24

As the days pressed on, Rebecca was slowly but surely improving.

Each day Charlie would come to the hospital and visit with her, and he noticed definite signs of progress.

It was hard work for Rebecca, but she was determined to get herself well so that she could function on her own and finally marry Charlie.

The doctors recommended that Rebecca would soon be strong enough, and it was time to tell her about her pregnancy, before her belly starts to grow and she feels the twins moving around inside of her.

Rebecca's father ultimately decided that since Charlie was the father of one of the babies, that he should be the one to tell her, and now that she was out of her coma, it would be difficult explaining why one of the babies was not his.

They were trying to shelter her from the fact that she had been raped minutes after she conceived Charlie's baby.

No, that would be too much to put on her.

As it stood she remembered nothing about Oscar or the vicious assault. It would be much better for her to just believe that both twins were Charlies, and later if she ever got her memory back, he could deal with it then.

Even the doctors were in agreement in keeping Rebecca in the dark about the rape.

It could be too traumatic for her well-being if she remembers.

Rebecca's father, who was still in control of Rebecca's health decisions, had devised a plan to get rid of Oscar's baby once she was born.

He collaborated with the doctors that when the babies were coming, they were going to sedate Rebecca during her final minutes of labor, and claim that Oscar's baby was still born and quickly remove it from the delivery room.

Then continue on with the plan to send the baby off to Peru, where she would disappear and be raised by the nuns in the monastery.

It was a devious plan, but it sounded good to Charlie too, considering he would have to be in on it.

But what other choice did he have?

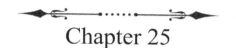

Chapter 25

A month had passed and Rebecca was getting even stronger, and was scheduled to be released from the hospital.

She regained most of her speech, although she was still having trouble with certain words longer than two syllables, and was carefully walking around the hospital with a walker.

Her brain functions were improving, except for occasional struggling to remember people's names and distant memories.

It was a blessing though, that she still had no memory whatsoever of Oscar's horrific assault, and everyone was happy about that.

It was her final day in the hospital and Charlie informed her that he had a surprise for her.

He drove over to the hospital and helped her pack her things from her room, and then he began wheeling her down the long hallways to the discharge exit.

She sat there proudly, carrying her bouquets of flowers as he pushed her along.

Nurses and doctors popped out to see her off and it was a happy occasion for all of them.

She was curious about her surprise though, as Charlie helped her into his new pick up truck.

He placed all her belongings into the truck's rear bed and closed the folding bed cover, and off they went.

She sat there quietly with the window down, just breathing the fresh air and letting the sun shine on her face.

Charlie carefully drove out of the parking lot and continued on as he firmly held Rebecca's hand.

He meandered down a few side streets and merged onto the highway heading to Castle Rock, a suburban town south of Denver.

After traveling for about twenty minutes, he exited the highway and continued on for a few more miles when he suddenly turned onto a long gravel driveway that led to a ranch spread.

He pulled to the end of the driveway and stopped the car next to the old rustic house.

"Why are we stopping here at this farm, Charlie?" Rebecca inquired.

"I have a surprise for you, Rebecca. This is our new home," Charlie softly stated.

Rebecca was flabbergasted and didn't know what to say.

"Our old place was unbearable and I thought we could use a fresh start considering that we might be starting a family soon," Charley coyly stated.

Rebecca blushed at the notion since she was still unaware that she was pregnant.

Charlie jumped out of the car and then helped Rebecca out, since she was still weak and using crutches to hobble along.

They both stood there as Rebecca smiled and absorbed the ranch.

In front of them was a white washed cottage style farmhouse with a flower garden on the side, and a porch with a swinging bench.

The front yard was mostly overgrown with weeds, and fenced in by a faded and peeling white picket fence.

On the other side of the gravel driveway, approximately 20 yards away, there was a natural weathered wood barn with several empty horse stalls and a hay loft above.

There was also a rusted push lawn mower covered with cobwebs, and an old antiquated farm tractor with an archaic large spiked hay loader attached to the front of it.

And next to the barn was an old dilapidated windmill, that hadn't worked in years, but still managed to rotate a few unbalanced revolutions when a storm blew in.

Rebecca was in jubilant shock, and she hugged Charlie and told him that she loved the place!

"I couldn't bring you back to Cedar street, and I wanted a fresh start for the both of us. Come on, I want to show you more," Charlie proudly stated.

He scooped her up as if she were a bride and carried her onto the porch and sat her down on an old swing bench that was hanging from the porch ceiling, made from old locust wood branches. It looked uncomfortable, but had a cushion on the seat to ease the pain.

"Before I bring you inside, I want to really make this official," Charlie firmly stated.

"He got down on his knee and reached into his pocket, removing the ring box which contained her engagement ring.

Rebecca began to tear up and weep in anticipation, as she knew what was inside that green velvet ring box.

"Rebecca, I've been holding on to this ring since the day of the break in. I was planning on giving it to you that night, but obviously things didn't work out as I planned. I know you heard me while you were in your coma, but I want to make it official. 'Rebecca Kannon, will you marry me?'" Charlie beamed.

Rebecca began to cry as Charlie placed the ring on her ring finger.

It fit perfectly, just as the two of them.

"Yes, Charlie Rama, I would be honored to be your wife," Rebecca cheerfully replied, and they kissed.

Whatever tragic hurdles they had hit were now behind them, except for one more issue.

It was time to tell her about the twins.

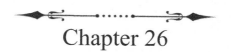

Chapter 26

The sun was slowly setting as the couple sat together on their porch swing, and they talked about their plans of getting married as the rickety bench gently swung back and forth.

Rebecca was saddened by the fact that her mother would not be there, but glad that her father would be, and that he would be walking her down the aisle and giving her away to the love of her life, Charlie.

"Come on, I want to show you the house," exclaimed Charlie and he scooped Rebecca up again and carried his bride over the threshold and into the house.

It was small and quaint, and in need of a lot of repair, but it was theirs and a place to call home.

"I love it Charlie, this is perfect for the two of us," Rebecca cheerfully stated as she crutched her way throughout their new home. She paused at the base of the staircase with her crutches, then turned into the downstairs adjacent bedroom and noticed that the bedroom furniture was all brand new.

Charlie had an idea of what she was thinking;

"How could he afford all of this on his meager salary while working at the drugstore?"

"Rebecca, another part of the surprise is that I have a new job. Mr. Maxwell, the owner of the drug store, retired and he sold me the business. I made some changes and updated things and now business is

booming! You won't have to go back to work when the babies come," Charlie blurted out.

Rebecca was thrilled by the news that Charlie had bought the pharmacy, but suddenly her demeanor changed and she became concerned.

"Babies? Geez Charlie, I think it's a little early to be talking about kids! Actually I'm not even sure I want kids for a while. We have plenty of time for that sort of talk," Rebecca stated.

Charlie sat Rebecca down on the bed and placed her two hands into his, and he took a deep breath.

"I have something important to tell you, Rebecca," and he tightened his grip and looked her straight in her eyes.

She became anxious and her face went blank.

Charlie continued;

"I know you don't remember much about the night we were attacked, but I was wondering if there is anything prior to the assault that you might remember?"

Rebecca thought for a moment and replied;

"I remember that we had a romantic evening planned that night and that I was waiting for you to come home, and I fell asleep. There is nothing else there, I'm sorry Charlie."

Charlie took another deep breath and sighed.

"Rebecca, we went to choir practice together that afternoon and you decided the time was right for us to make love together, and so we had a romantic dinner planned for that evening. I was late because I was picking up your engagement ring from the jewelry store, and I also picked up flowers and Chinese takeout food for our romantic evening.

When I got home you had fallen asleep in bed wearing sexy lingerie and looking so beautiful. I gently woke you up and we started kissing and we instantly became passionate. It was so beautiful to finally consummate our love for each other," Charlie softly stated.

Rebecca smiled and sadly stated that she did not remember the love making, but was confident if Charlie said they did it, they did it.

"Thank you for sharing that with me Charlie, the doctor said that whenever I feel ready we can start having sex. But first, I think I need to see a doctor about some sort of birth control, don't you think so too, Charlie?" Rebecca cautiously stated.

Charlie began rubbing his face with his two hands as sweat began permeating all over his body, and Rebecca could see that something was wrong.

"What's going on, Charlie?" she gravely inquired.

"Rebecca, that first and only time ever that we made love. You must have been ovulating, because you are pregnant now and are carrying twins," Charlie nervously blurted out.

Rebecca was stunned and in a state of shock!

After all that she had gone through, and no one had ever told her that she was pregnant until now!

She shoved Charlie away and hastily crutched herself back to the truck and got in.

"I want to go back to my fathers house!" she shouted at Charlie as he followed closely behind her.

"I'm sorry Rebecca, I know we should have told you earlier but the doctors felt that you needed more time!" Charlie pleaded.

She began to calm down as she sat in the truck and began thinking things through.

"How can it be? The first time we ever had intercourse and I got pregnant?! And not just with just one baby but twins! Are you sure it's not a mistake?!!" Rebecca exclaimed.

"Believe me Rebecca, no one was more surprised than me, and stranger things have happened regarding pregnancies. They did an ultrasound at the hospital and verified that you are pregnant. It must have been God's will Rebecca," Charlie stated.

Rebecca began to soften and realized that maybe Charlie was right, it was God's will and maybe this was just part of God's plan for them.

Rebecca opened the truck door and began to cry.

"I'm so sorry Charlie. Together, from our love we made a baby, actually two babies! I knew I felt my body was changing but I thought it was because of the attack or the coma. Now I understand why I have this "bump" growing in my stomach. I thought I had a cancerous tumor growing inside of me and I was starting to freak out!" Rebecca jokingly stated.

Charlie was relieved that the cat was finally out of the bag, however that dark secret that she was also carrying Oscar's spawn was still hovering over him like a giant lightning charged thunder cloud.

Hopefully she'll never find out, but it was going to be difficult since the tabloids were all over the story.

Charlie thought that keeping her isolated at the farm with no television or newspapers would help, and it was only for another six months. Difficult but not impossible.

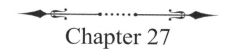

Chapter 27

The guests waited with sheer anticipation as the church bells clamored loudly, swinging briskly way up high in the church's tall steeple, and their wedding was underway.

It was a little complicated, but Rebecca's father was walking her down the aisle and then changing into his minister role and was performing the wedding ceremony.

The church was filled to capacity and they were surrounded by their families and friends.

Rebecca began her march down the aisle, and the guests rose and turned to see her in her beautiful white sequined gown and veil.

There were a pair of twin toddler flower girls marching in front of her, tossing rose pedals as the giant pipe organ blared the wedding march.

However, one of the twins was behaved and orderly, but the other was behaving badly and mischievous as she threw the flower petals at the guests.

Charlie was up on the podium with his best man, as he proudly waited for his beautiful bride to come to him.

Her dress was long and glamorous, and her veil was flowing and elegant.

It covered her face and blocked her vision going forward, and she strained to see where she was going.

Her father led her up the steps to the podium where they met Charlie, and he took her hand and smiled.

"I love you, babe." he warmly stated.

As they both approached the altar, Rebecca didn't notice her father rummaging off to the side, and putting on his minister's robe.

She stood there silently with Charlie, unable to see a thing until she heard these words from her minister father;

"You may lift her veil now, Charlie."

Charlie turned to her and delicately lifted her veil, and then instantly she could see the world clearly.

She saw Charlie looking so handsome in his pure white tuxedo suit, and then she turned to face her father, the minister.

Rebecca suddenly became shocked and mortified, and she placed her hands over her face, trembling and screaming at the top of her lungs!

The minister who was there at the altar was not her father!

It was that monster Oscar, the crazed psychopath wearing her fathers minister robe! And he was holding a bible in one hand and his bloody butcher's cleaver in the other!!

Oscar had found her!

He raised his glistening butcher's cleaver and started swinging it wildly as he instantly began chasing after her!

She was frightened to death and tried to escape his wrath, but she was running as fast as she could, with her blood splattered wedding gown and veil flailing behind her, however she seemed to be running to nowhere!

Oscar had grabbed hold and wrapped her trailing veil around his arm and was pulling her closer, as he maniacally laughed and raised his weapon to deliver a decisive decapitating stroke!

He swung his razor sharp cleaver toward her neck, just as Rebecca unleashed a blood curdling scream!!

Then, Rebecca suddenly felt a shaking sensation as Charlie was trying to awaken her from her terrifying dream!

She was soaked with sweat and her heart was pounding.

"Charlie, I had the most awful dream!!" she cried.

"Relax honey, it was just a dream. It's okay, I'm here with you, now," Charlie softly stated as he consoled her.

"It was terrible, Charlie! It was our wedding day and we were at the church. I was going down the aisle and there were these two twin little girls throwing flower petals in front of me, one was good and throwing red pedals and the other was bad and throwing black pedals and cursing at the guests. As I continued down the aisle, my veil was so dense I couldn't see what was going on. It was as if I was in the dark about something. And so I marched up to the podium where I met you under the altar. You lifted my veil and that's when I realized that the minister was not my father but Oscar, the psychopath and he was going to chop off my head!! What do you think that all meant, Charlie?!" Rebecca exclaimed.

Charlie fumbled with his words, but assured her that it was just a meaningless dream, and that their wedding the following day was going to be spectacular.

Unbeknown to her, was that she was being kept in the dark and that she was carrying two different babies in her womb, and Oscar was responsible for one of them.

"Tomorrow is our wedding day, Rebecca. And it will be spectacular! Don't you worry about a thing. That nut case Oscar is locked up and he'll never see the light of day, ever again. Tomorrow you will be my bride, and tomorrow night you will be my wife," Charlie gushed.

"And tomorrow you will be my groom, and tomorrow night you will be my husband. And I'll be ready to make love with you again, Charlie." Rebecca seductively whispered.

Charlie looked over at a crucifix that was hanging on the wall and shouted;

"Thank you Jesus!" and Rebecca laughed.

She cuddled up next to him and they held each other as Charlie drifted off to sleep, but Rebecca had a gut feeling that something was going on, and that no one was telling her.

Maybe she was just being paranoid.

But maybe not.

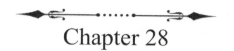

Chapter 28

Their church wedding was small, only a few friends and family were invited.

It was a private and secret ceremony since no one wanted the paparazzi crashing in and spilling the beans about who's baby Rebecca was really carrying.

Oddly, Rebecca wasn't showing much at about 4 months, but things were about to change during her second trimester.

After their church ceremony, there was a small reception and then they immediately flew out to Costa rica for their honeymoon, at a secluded beach resort.

Their honeymoon was short and sweet, and despite their overindulgence of sexual activity, Rebecca still had no memory of that horrific evening with Oscar, and Charlie was making up for lost time.

When they finally returned back to Castle Rock, Rebecca got to work decorating the nursery while Charlie returned back to work at the drugstore.

It was difficult for Charlie to keep the secret about the assault and Oscar's baby, and the fact that she was going to disappear right after birth.

But everyone felt it was for the best, and seeing one baby that resembled Charlie, and then the other which possibly resembled Oscar might tip off Rebecca that the babies had two different fathers, and she might figure out what happened.

The weeks and then months flew by, and Rebecca's belly was expanding.

She often told Charlie that it felt as if there was a war going on inside her belly, with the two babies carrying on.

But Charlie nonchalantly passed it off and told her that they were probably playing tag.

But the fact of the matter was, he was extremely nervous and worried sick, and he could only imagine that Oscar's child was beating the living pulp out of his daughter, and there wasn't a thing he could do about it. All he could do was pray and hope for the best.

Rebecca was getting excited with the idea of being a mother, and she was spending most of her days preparing for her children and shopping for her soon to be newborn twins.

It began pulling on Charlie's heart strings, knowing how devastated Rebecca will be when she learns that one of the babies will be still born, but he firmly believed in his heart that it was for the best.

As soon as she holds their "good" child, God will heal her and hopefully she will quickly recover from her loss.

Her father ultimately signed the papers, and if anyone is going to be blamed if she ever found out, it was going to be Mr. Kannon.

After all, they weren't married at the time and her father was her next of kin and calling all of her heath decisions, and it was all his idea to get rid of the baby.

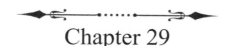

Chapter 29

It was just past midnight and the howling winds of a violent storm were brewing outside of their farm house.

The dark ominous clouds opened and pelting rain pummeled from the sky along with violent lightning bolts and loud booming thunder.

Rebecca was restless and that's when she felt her first powerful contraction.

She shook Charlie from his sleep and shouted;

"Charlie, it's time to go to the hospital, I'm having contractions!"

Charlie nearly fell out of the bed as his nerves got the better of him.

He frantically stumbled around the bedroom putting his clothes on over his pajamas as Rebecca was calmly getting dressed.

He managed to remember her hospital suitcase after he had already helped her into his truck, and then they recklessly raced off to the hospital!

Charlie quickly called her father, and told him to get to the hospital so that they could "get things ready" for the delivery.

Rebecca's water suddenly broke, and she was now having severe contractions and they were coming every fifteen seconds!

Tensions were escalating as they were both beginning to worry that she was not going to make it

to the hospital, and she was going to give birth right there in the truck!

"Hurry up you son of a bitch, piece of shit!! I'm in so much pain, and you did this to me you ass hole!!" she screamed at Charlie.

This wasn't the Rebecca he had known, but he understood that she was in pain and that labor could change his wife's demeanor.

"Hold on, we're almost there!" Charlie exclaimed.

He jumped his car over the boulevard median and was heading directly toward the oncoming traffic, and just before a tractor trailer truck nearly collided with them, he cut his wheel and went crashing over the curb and drove through the landscaping shrubs and grass, into the emergency room parking lot!!

When they finally arrived at the hospital, Charlie ran into the lobby screaming that his wife was going to have a baby any second!

A group of nurses and an intern raced out to the truck with a gurney, and they quickly assisted Rebecca onto the stretcher!

She was screaming in pain and in agony, and managed to unleash several more inappropriate profanities directed toward Charlie as they rushed her off into the hospital.

The medical team quickly wheeled her directly into a delivery room, where there was a team of doctors prepared and waiting for her.

They immediately sedated her, and she suddenly became drowsy and couldn't keep her eyes open, and she was put to sleep.

The doctors quickly moved her into the operating room and were preparing to perform a cesarean

delivery, but no one was really comfortable with what they might be pulling out of her womb, and they were all preparing themselves for the worst.

Although no one really believed that Oscar's newborn daughter was going to come flying out of Rebecca with a chainsaw or a butcher's cleaver, they were still concerned that they could be under attack, since after all, it was Oscar's larvae they were letting out.

Charlie was a nervous wreck as he waited in the hospital lounge, and he was having dire second thoughts about taking Oscar's baby away from Rebecca, knowing she would be devastated by the loss of one of her children.

But the plan was in motion and there was no backing out now.

The doctors had just removed one of the babies and she seemed to be totally fine and healthy.

A beautiful brown haired baby which they assumed was Charlies.

She was placed in a heated incubator while they removed the other baby who seemed gangly and had a full head of bright red hair, which they presumed was obviously Oscars since he was also a redhead.

The nurse placed baby #2 into another incubator as the doctors began sewing up Rebecca.

An identification card was placed on the first incubator stating the generic name "Baby girl Rama #1" and then another card on the second incubator stating "Baby girl Rama #2".

Then two nurses quickly rolled the two incubators off to the nursery, where the two babies would be looked after until adoption administrators from the

Peruvian social service agency were to arrive, to take Oscar's child, and transport her to the monastery in Peru.

When the two babies arrived at the nursery, they were quickly bathed and then bundled up, and a DNA profile was performed on both babies.

A pair of teenage nurses' aids were assigned to tend and bottle feed the newborn babies.

The girls were rambling on about their upcoming high school prom dates and the lavish gowns which they had purchased for the occasion.

They were so consumed with their conversation about the prom and their boyfriends, that they were not paying much attention to the babies, and most importantly, which baby came from which of the incubators, and so they inadvertently mixed them up!

When they suddenly realized that neither of them had any idea which baby was which, they were concerned that they would be reprimanded and get in trouble with the head nurse for mixing them up.

Neither of the nurses' aids had any knowledge that minutes later one of the babies was going to be taken away by the Peruvian authorities, and so they assumed that both babies were going to the same home anyway, so it didn't really seem to matter.

Tragically they placed the babies back into the wrong incubators where now Oscar's baby was returned into Baby girl Rama #1's incubator and Charlie's baby into Baby girl Rama #2's incubator.

As the two teenage nurses' aids were leaving, one of the girls jokingly picked up a marker and scribbled "Wonder" on Baby #1's identification card, which was taped to the front of the incubator.

The girls quickly left the two babies as they comfortably slept, and continued out of the nursery, still rambling on about their prom dates, just minutes before the two Peruvian social service agents arrived.

They were hardened and serious middle aged hispanic women, dressed in gray polyester pantsuits, and they were officially there to confiscate Oscar's baby.

The lab had just phoned up the DNA results to the nursery's nurses station and confirmed that Baby girl Rama #2 was in fact the Oscar Demento child.

The nurse reaffirmed that it was baby #2 and then she proceeded to the nursery and informed the Peruvian social service agents to take baby #2.

The agents, assisted by a nurse, quickly packaged some travel items into a diaper bag and then they confiscated the baby, and then proceeded to leave, carrying the tiny newborn baby in an infant car seat as they left the nursery.

Charlie's nerves were getting the better of him, and he decided to leave the recovery room and rush off to the nursery to see his child.

He was beginning to have a guilty conscience, in that he was in kahoots with Rebecca's father and the doctors, and for going along with the big lie that one of her twins had died during childbirth.

He felt it was a sin, and that he would ultimately go to hell for going along with it.

His high morals and religious beliefs suddenly got the better of him, and he suddenly decided he couldn't go through with it and had to stop the plan.

The two Peruvian social service agents passed by him in the hallway as they were leaving with his baby.

He had no idea who they were and that they were transporting *his* child to the monastery, and that they had mistakenly left Oscar's child for them to raise as their own.

When Charlie arrived at the nursery he only saw the one red haired baby, Baby girl Rama #1 in the incubator, and the other baby was already gone!

He frantically grabbed one of the nurses and asked her where the other baby was, and she replied;

"They just left with her!"

Charlie ran out of the nursery and took the stairwell down to the parking garage.

He noticed the two hispanic women putting an infant car seat into the back of a black SUV and he rushed over towards them.

"Hey, you with the baby! Stop!!" he shouted.

The two women froze and thought that possibly Charlie was an American kidnapper or a carjacker, and quickly scrambled into their car and locked the doors.

Charlie pleaded with them to give him the baby back, but they were cold and calculating and stated that Rebecca's father and the mother had signed the papers, and it was too late!

They quickly started their SUV and proceeded to dash away as Charlie dove up onto the hood of their vehicle, and he clung onto the windshield wipers as he sprawled himself across the hood of the vehicle.

The SUV began racing through the parking garage, swerving side to side as they tried to shake Charlie off.

Charlie was determined and held tight as the driver continued driving erratically, despite the fact that there was a newborn baby in the car.

As they raced towards the exit an onslaught of security cars suddenly raced in and blocked the exitway.

The SUV screeched to a stop and the security officers swarmed the car.

"Open up the door! You took the wrong baby!" an officer shouted.

The two women were bewildered and opened up the door.

Charlie quickly took possession of who they thought to be Oscar's baby, but was in fact his own child.

"We noticed on the nursery surveillance video that the nurses' aids switched up the two babies by mistake!" the officer exclaimed.

"Well, we have paperwork that says we are taking "a" baby, so hand over the other one!" the social worker demanded.

"I'm the father of both babies! You're not taking either of my daughters! Those papers were forged by Rebecca's father, Mr. Kannon!" Charlie insisted.

The social workers were confused and stated that the mothers signature was also on the document dated seven months ago.

"How could she sign a document seven months ago when she was in a coma! You touch my other

daughter and I'll have you arrested for kidnapping!"
Charlie exclaimed.

The two women looked at each other and were obviously frustrated, then they conceded and backed down and allowed Charlie to leave with the baby.

He dashed over to the parking garage stairwell and charged back up to the maternity ward.

He heard Rebecca crying in her room and her father was there, breaking the news to her that the second one of her twins, didn't make it, and was born dead!

Charlie continued on, lugging the baby in the car seat, and was desperately running back to the nursery!

He quickly removed the infant from the car seat and carefully placed her back into her incubator, and then raced back to Rebecca's room, pushing the baby along in front of him.

"It was a mistake! The baby is alive! Both babies are fine!" Charlie shouted, as he pushed the incubator into her room.

Her father was stunned and gave Charlie a nasty look of disgust, and then abruptly left the room.

Rebecca was still a bit dazed and uncomfortable from the cesarean section, and she was sad and hysterically crying as she held and nurtured her surviving baby, who they planned to name Grace, and the second baby out was to be named, Wanda.

However, she lit up when she saw Charlie and her other baby come charging into her room.

They mixed up the babies in the nursery, Rebecca! This is Grace.

The baby you are holding is… is… Wanda!

Rebecca then noticed the baby's name card on the incubator;

"Baby girl Rama #1" and saw that someone had scribbled "Wonder" on it with a marker, and she thought it was divine and meaningful.

And so she smiled and said;

"No Charlie. This is baby Wonder, Wonder Rama...The child of wonder."

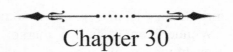

Chapter 30

The notion of Wonder dispatching Grace in the womb was sensationalized, and both babies were nothing out of the ordinary.

The tabloids gradually lost interest, and the Las Vegas show boating ended.

Occasionally there were tabloid photographers, trying to catch a glimpse of the twins, but Charlie would run them off the farm when he caught them.

But they were bold and sneaky, and often hid in the woods with telescopic camera lenses, trying to catch a shot of the twins.

It was difficult for Charlie at first, to show any compassion or love for Oscar's baby.

But over time he actually grew to love her.

"It wasn't her fault that she was conceived the way she was," he thought and after all, she was still half Rebecca's child and he believed that her goodness would dominate and overcome any evil in the child.

Both children were growing up and were equally showered with love, and they began to develop with no cognitive or psychotic issues other than Grace was a little timid and more reluctant to explore her surroundings, where Wonder was more outgoing and curious.

It wasn't until the babies started preschool when they began noticing a change in Wonders behavior.

She was very protective of Grace, especially if any of the other children were taking advantage or being harsh toward her.

Wonder would quickly step in and stand up for her sister.

If ever there was an incident of unkindness towards Grace, Wonder would become stern and clench her fists in a manner that was usually enough to send the message to stop messing with her sister or else.

Rebecca never regained her memory of that night or the horrific assault, and that was just fine with Charlie.

Their lives were happy and complete now, and their home was filled with love and religion.

The relationship between Charlie and Rebecca's father however was strained, and he could not accept the fact that Wonder was his bastard grandchild, and he was still angry with Charlie for interfering with the adoption procedure, and his effort to get rid of Wonder.

Mr. Kannon believed deep in his heart that Wonder was evil like her father, and someday that "Silicon switch inside her head, was going to switch to overload," as exemplified in the song by the punk rock band the Boomtown Rats, about how a California teenager named Brenda Spencer woke up one Monday morning, and decided to start shooting her gun and killing children and faculty who were attending the elementary school across the street from her house.

After the police apprehended her, they asked her why she did it, and her response was;

"Because, I don't like Mondays."

No one knew for sure what was going to happen and if someday Wonder was going to evolve into Oscar, but beside her over protective nature, she seemed to be a loving and caring normal little redheaded girl.

Grace on the other hand was sometimes moody and introverted.

She preferred to look at books rather than go outside and explore.

Then something happened one early spring afternoon, when the girls were about 12 years old.

Wonder raced into Grace's bedroom, and took her sister by the hand and told her she wanted to show her something that she had discovered by the fringe of the pasture.

Grace was reluctant and had to be prodded, but she finally agreed to go.

Unbeknown to them there was a tabloid photographer hidden in the brush and was following them, hoping to score a photograph of the pair.

Wonder craftily led her sister off, down through a trail in the woods to the pasture, and they continued walking along the edge of the field until they came upon a large rotting tree stump.

It was situated on the fringe of the pasture, and next to a running brook.

Grace was skeptical and complained that she had been dragged all the way out there to see a tree stump?

Wonder's face became stern as she picked up a large rock and crept up behind Grace.

"It's not about the tree stump, silly. It's what's behind it, on the other side, that's what I want to show you! Lean over the top and look to the other side," Wonder maniacally giggled.

Grace leaned over the top of the tree stump, stretching over to see what Wonder was talking about, as Wonder raised the boulder over her head with her two hands, and stared at the back of Grace's head.

As Grace peeked over the stump she saw that there was a shallow grave dug into the earth, which was mostly concealed under the stump.

And then Wonder whispered to her;

"Lean over even more, for a better look!" coaxing her sister closer to the pit!

Grace peered over the stump, straining as she was stretching over it to see, as Wonder was directly behind her with the boulder raised high above her head, and she was focused on the back of Grace's skull!

"Just a little bit farther, Gracey." Wonder coaxed.

Grace strained to see what was so interesting to Wonder, when it finally hit her!

And then to Grace's amazement, she saw that there were two small black bear cubs, sleeping in the den, on a bed of dried grass.

"Oh my, they are so cute!" Grace exclaimed.

"Don't touch them! If the mother smells a human's scent on them she will abandon her young," Wonder stated.

Then she turned and tossed the boulder into the brook, which created a loud splash in the water.

The sound of the splash abruptly awoke the cubs and startled them, and they instantly began crying out in distress for their mother!

Then suddenly, the girls heard a loud rustling tumult in the woods, as if a bull was charging towards them!

It was apparent that the cub's mother was nearby and heard her cubs crying out in distress, and was rushing back to her den to protect her young.

Grace began screaming hysterically when she realized that an angry mother bear was coming after them!

"Don't scream and don't run! Lay down and play dead or you'll get mauled!!" Wonder exclaimed.

But Grace was panic stricken and desperate to get away, and she started running across the pasture as fast as she could!

The big black sow zeroed in on Grace and took off after her, as she perceived that she had confiscated her two young cubs!

The enraged bear bolted past Wonder who was lying on the ground pretending to be dead, and she chased after Grace, who was screaming wildly as the bear was charging after her!

Wonder's heart began to pound and something was coming over her.

She began to swell and she became empowered.

Her adrenalin began charging her blood vessels and she suddenly became superhuman!

She instinctively jumped up off the ground and bolted right after the bear, who was quickly gaining on her sister!

With phenomenal speed, she bore down on the bear and dove through the air just seconds before the bear was about to grab hold of Grace with her razor sharp claws!

She clamped herself onto the enormous bear's back, and put her arm around the bear's throat and began to tighten her grip.

The bear frantically struggled to get her off her back, and began rolling and tumbling through the tall pasture grass as Wonder tightened her choking grip on her, and began strangling the bear until the sow finally collapsed and became unconscious.

Wonder released her hold just prior to completely suffocating the bear and was careful not to kill it.

Grace stood there petrified as she had just witnessed the phenomenal event.

Her sister had saved her life by doing what seemed impossible.

She subdued a full blown raging mother bear in its tracks.

"Are you okay, Grace!" Wonder exclaimed as she tried to calm herself down.

"How did you do that, Wonder?!!" Grace exclaimed.

"I don't know! When I saw you in danger all I knew was I had to protect you, and something changed inside of me. And it happened instantly," Wonder stated.

"Let's get out of here before that bear wakes up!" Grace declared.

"Grace, please don't bring this up to Mom and Dad. I'll get in trouble for not knowing better and putting us in a dangerous situation," pleaded Wonder.

Grace understood and they held hands as they quickly left the pasture and returned home.

When the coast was clear, the sleazy photographer emerged from the forest gripping his precious camera as if it were the holy grail.

He quickly ran off, stumbling over himself while carrying his soon to be prized photograph of Wonder, chasing down the enraged bear and single handedly subduing the beast.

The cat was out of the bag, and it now seemed that Wonder had inherited her fathers enlarged hypothalamus, amygdala and enlarged adrenal glands.

She too had the ability to become supernatural, just like Oscar, her paternal father.

And now the world was going to hear about it.

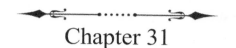

Chapter 31

Charlie usually arrived at the drugstore each morning at about 6 AM, just in time to bring in deliveries and set up the prescriptions for the oncoming day.

He parked his pickup truck in his usual spot, way in the back parking lot to leave the closer spaces for his customers.

On his way in to open the store, he passed the stacks of daily newspapers and tabloids left by his distributor for him to stock the news stand in his drug store.

He instantly noticed the front page of a tabloid newspaper with an odd and blurry black and white photograph.

The headline read;

"WONDER RAMA IS OSCAR'S SPAWN!!"

Charlie quickly ripped the paper from the stack and was mortified when upon closer examination, he saw that the front page picture was of his daughter, Wonder!

And she was taking down a full sized black bear as it chased after Grace!

He quickly read the article and then, in disgust he scooped up the entire stack of the papers and threw them into his dumpster.

He had no idea that Wonder was secretly harboring the fact that she had supernatural powers.

He firmly believed that eventually Rebecca would either see the tabloid or she would be confronted by more tabloid reporters, and so he decided it was time to tell Rebecca what really happened that horrific night.

It will be difficult, but he had to tell her the truth, that he was not actually Wonder's biological father, and that she was sexually assaulted only minutes after they had consummated their love for each other.

And that Oscar Demento was, in fact, Wonder's real biological father.

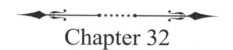

Chapter 32

The day dragged on as that ominous dark cloud hovered over Charlie.

But as the day's end neared, he was ready to get things out into the open, and not only reveal the truth to Rebecca, but to Grace and Wonder too.

Wonder had to be confused and afraid that something was wrong with her, and sooner or later, one of her friends who would have seen the tabloid was going to spill the beans to her and her classmates.

Especially since it was now on every newsstand and supermarket shelf in Denver.

It had to be done and there was no better time than tonight.

It was supper time when Charlie rolled into their driveway.

The girls were outside playing basketball, shooting baskets at the old hoop that was nailed over the barns front door.

They both enthusiastically rushed over to greet their dad, and were happy that he was home after not seeing him all day long.

Rebecca was inside preparing food and called out the kitchen window that supper was ready, and they should all come inside and eat while the food was hot.

The dinner was awkward and there was only a little if any small talk at the table, as Charlie was obviously stressed out about bringing up the issue at hand.

"What's wrong, Charlie?" Rebecca finally inquired as she began clearing the table.

"Charlie picked up his ice cold glass of lemonade and took a long drink, and then pressed the cool condensation on the glass against his forehead and said;

"Girls, can you go back outside and play? I have to talk to your mother about something important."

Rebecca grew concerned and she nodded for the girls to leave.

"What's going on Charlie?" Rebecca nervously inquired as she sat back down at the kitchen table, across from Charlie.

"Rebecca, I have to talk to you about the night we were assaulted. We were all scared when you were in that deep coma, and when you miraculously woke up, we weren't sure how well you were going to be. Everyone including me, your father and the doctors all thought that it was a blessing that you had no memory of that horrific night, and everyone thought it would be better for you not to remember," Charlie nervously stated.

Rebecca's face began to tighten as she was growing concerned about where Charlie was going with this.

Charlie continued;

"The time has come that I am reluctantly going to have to tell you about that night, Rebecca. I've been keeping you isolated on the farm, but this morning I saw a tabloid newspaper that is exposing things, and I need to tell you before someone confronts you about it, or you see it for yourself."

"No!! I don't want to hear it, Charlie! Everything is perfect now, and it will ruin everything!" Rebecca exclaimed as she put her hands over her ears.

Charlie knew that he had to tell her and going forward, whatever was going to happen was now in God's hands.

"Rebecca, you trust me right?" Charlie softly said.

Rebecca cautiously nodded her head and removed her hands from her ears.

"We love each other no matter what happened that night, and we have two beautiful little girls that we both love and adore. That tragic night was supposed to be beautiful for us. Just me and you celebrating. It was the night that you finally decided to give yourself to me, and it was also the night I had finally paid off your engagement ring. I had stopped off for Chineses take out and I hid the ring in a fortune cookie. When I got home you had fallen asleep on the bed and when I woke you, you were so beautiful and we couldn't resist each other, and so we made love."

Rebecca began to blush as Charlie smiled and continued;

"Afterwards we were laying in bed and I thought it was a good opportunity to ask you to marry me, so I hopped up off the bed and that's when I heard a noise coming from the kitchen.

Without any warning that maniac burst into our bedroom and I was fighting for our lives.

But he was too strong and powerful. Stronger than anyone or anything I had ever encountered. He was slashing me and beating the crap out of me, but I didn't care, all I wanted to do was protect you. He finally threw me out the bedroom window and I fell

two stories on top of my car and I was knocked unconscious. That's about where I ended my version of the story that I told you in the hospital, but there was more that I kept from you."

Rebecca began to brace herself, as Charlie continued;

"It all happened so fast, that you never had a chance to get out of there, and then he turned his attention to you. He violently assaulted you and if it wasn't for that US Marshal showing up when he did, that psychopath would have killed you.

That madman that attacked us was Oscar Demento.

The police said that he was infatuated with you from the moment he saw you in the courtroom. He noticed your vanity license plate when you left the courthouse and was able to obtain your address through a police radio, only it was your parents address that was on file. When he showed up at your parents' doorstep, it was you he was after, but instead he sadistically murdered your mother just for the hell of it."

Rebecca began to cry and she was losing control.

"So it was that maniac Oscar Demento that beat me to near death? Why didn't you tell me, Charlie? I could have handled that," Rebecca cried.

"There's more, Rebecca. Oscar sexually assaulted you while you were unconscious and he left his seed in you. I'm sorry to have to tell you this, but you became pregnant with both mine and Oscar's children. Grace is my daughter and Wonder is Oscar's daughter."

Rebecca's whole world began to spin out of control and she collapsed. Charlie quickly caught her and

placed her on the couch, and then he quickly ran to the kitchen sink and got a cold wet face cloth and placed it on her forehead.

She just laid there on the couch, just blankly staring at the ceiling, speechless and pressing the cool face cloth against her forehead.

Charlie continued;

"At first having Oscar's baby inside of you was appalling to me and your father. He signed papers and forged your signature to send Wonder off for adoption once she was born, and that's why he told you she died.

My conscience got the better of me and even though Oscar was her father, you were her mother and I couldn't lie to you.

Something happened in the nursery where the babies got mixed up and Grace was actually taken by the Peruvian social workers by mistake. After I caught up to them in the parking garage, I took Grace away from them, but they in turn said that they were coming for Wonder! I threatened them with a lawsuit, and I told them that your father had forged your signature and so they backed down.

Your father could never accept the fact that I interfered with getting rid of Wonder and that's why he stays away."

Rebecca was just lying on the couch and had drifted into a catatonic state, just trying to absorb all the information.

"How could you love Wonder, knowing Oscar is her father?" Rebecca suddenly exclaimed.

"It was hard at first. But when I held her and she clung to me we bonded. And when she called me Da-

da for the very first time, I fell in love with her. Even though I'm not her father, I am her dad, and I love her as much as I love Grace," Charlie stated.

"I'm so sorry Charlie, I wish I never took that courthouse job in the first place. I still don't remember anything from that horrific night, though. But I feel as if I want to kill myself knowing that, that beast Oscar Demento was inside of me, and honestly how could you touch me after you knew what he had done to me!" Rebecca tearfully stated.

"Because it wasn't your fault and I love you more than anything, that's how," Charlie replied.

Rebecca eked out a smile and took Charlie's hand.

Charlie then took a deep breath then continued;

"Well Rebecca, believe it or not, there's more. Wonder is a kind and gentle soul, not like her father. It seems though, that she did inherit her fathers adrenaline rush, and apparently last week she actually took down a black bear that was chasing after Grace in the pasture!"

Charlie then revealed the the front page of the newspaper, with the photograph of Wonder latched onto the back of the sow bear as it chased after Grace!

Rebecca couldn't believe her eyes as she recognised the clothes both girls were wearing.

"Wonder is nothing like that maniac, Oscar. She is kind and sweet and the most loving person I have ever known. More so than Grace!" Rebecca stated.

"I know Rebecca, she doesn't know that I know about her super-human strength and that's the next thing we need to talk about with the girls."

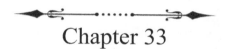

Chapter 33

It didn't seem real to Rebecca, what Charlie was telling her.

After all, she had no memory of the attack, and it didn't make any sense to her.

It was as if Charlie had told her that she was a Knight of the round table in medieval London in a prior life.

She had no memory of it, and it was hard for her to muster up any emotion for something she had no memory of.

Charlie opened the screen door from their kitchen and called out to the girls to come in.

The twins were up in the hayloft of the barn, investigating a feral cat's kitten nest, nestled in the corner of the loft, between a few bales of hay.

When they heard their father calling to them, they quickly climbed down the rickety ladder, and they carefully maneuvered around the long dangerous spears of the hay fork that was attached to the front of their farm tractor, and then they scurried off out of the barn and enthusiastically ran back to the house.

"Dad we found a Mom cat's nest and it's got six kittens inside! Can we keep one of the kittens, Daddy?!!" Wonder exclaimed.

"Of course you can, Girls. But first I need to talk to you both about something very serious, and I want

you to pay attention to me. I came across something today that I want to talk to you both about."

Charlie took a deep breath and then continued;

"Were you two involved in an incident with a bear, recently?" Charlie questioned.

The girls looked at each other and shrugged their shoulders, pretending not to know anything about a bear.

"Maybe this picture will refresh your memory," and Charlie revealed the newspaper photograph.

The twins were stunned that someone was actually out in the woods, and had captured that photograph without their knowledge.

Grace was the first to speak up, edging out Wonder, preventing her from confessing that she was actually the one to blame for bringing them to the bear den, and she would definitely get in trouble for endangering themselves.

"Well, 'we' were wandering around the pasture and 'we' found an old tree stump and then 'we' heard something making a funny noise. We discovered that there was a bear den with two baby cubs dug underneath the stump. We suddenly heard a lot of thrashing in the woods coming our way and it turned out to be the angry mother bear! Wonder told me to play dead but I was so scared I ran away. When the bear saw me running, she must have thought I was taking her cubs and she chased after me!! I felt that bear's breath on the back of my neck and she was ready to grab me from behind, and that's when Wonder saved me from the bear, Daddy!" tearfully stated Grace.

Wonder just stood there silently with her head bowed down to the floor, waiting for her punishment.

"Wonder, I know about your ability to become stronger. It's a condition where your brain organs trigger large amounts of a chemical in your body to turn you into a superhuman. You are stronger and faster than normal people. It only seems to come on when you are afraid or stressed out. You will have to learn to manage this, which it seems that you already have. I want you to know that it's a gift and if you use it for good things as God intended, you will be celebrated by everyone. But if it turns out to be bad, it will get you into trouble, like the person who was your other father," Charlie stated

"I'm sorry I didn't tell you about the bear, Daddy. But I was afraid that you would be angry with 'us' for finding the cubs. But what do you mean by 'my other father?'" questioned Wonder.

Charlie took a deep breath and explained;

"Wonder, sometimes things don't always go as planned and things happen. Right now you both are too young to understand things and you don't need to know everything. But 13 years ago your mom and I were visited by a stranger. We were very surprised by the situation, his name was Oscar. That's the moment when the Stork made a mistake and your mom got pregnant with the both of you. There must have been some sort of a mix up, but the Stork chose us to be your parents. Somehow, because Oscar was in our home at that moment, it confused the Stork when he was picking out babies, and because of that, you have different fathers. However, I want you to know that you are both my daughters and I love you exactly the

same. Wonder, you inherited this overactive adrenalin condition from him, but you don't have to worry about him trying to take you away from us because he died a long time ago," stated Charlie.

Charlie stopped there and believed that his roundabout explanation of how Rebecca became impregnated by "The Stork" would be sufficient and it would satisfy Wonder's pre pubescent mind about where babies came from.

At least for the time being.

Wonder stood there silently and emotionless, and then she took a deep breath and began to speak;

"Dad, I actually know what happened that night, and that mom was raped by that maniac who is my father, and he is in prison waiting for his appeals to run out and he will then be executed. It's all over the internet and it was easy to see from the reaction of my teachers and classmates, that I am supposed to be some sort of psychopathic freak, and a ticking time bomb just waiting to explode and start killing everyone. But I am nothing like my father, other than I have auburn hair and his overactive adrenal glands. I know you tried desperately to hide it from me, but I knew for a long time, since I was 7 years old, that I was different. I feel better now that it's out in the open. It was a terrible secret to keep inside, but thank God I have Grace to confide in and to be my best friend, and I have the best mom in the world. And you dad, for I never once felt that you loved me any less than my sister, I love my family with all my heart," Wonder confidently stated.

Charlie and Rebecca were overwhelmed and shocked that Wonder had already figured things out, and both twins had kept that secret for so long.

They shared a lengthy group hug where pent up tears were shed, and love and devotion engulfed them all.

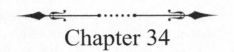

Chapter 34

The years of confinement were wreaking havoc on Oscar's demented mind.

Rather than accepting his fate and quietly doing his time until he was to be finally executed, he exercised his devious master-mind and continuously plotted out schemes so that he could possibly escape from his high security prison cell, and go on to feed his psychopathic thirst to kill once again.

But in reality he never had a chance due to the strength and sophistication of his confinement cell, and the implementation of the sleeping gas that was constantly used whenever they needed to gain access to his cell.

It was impossible for him to break out of there, but he wasn't going to stop trying.

Fifteen years had passed since he was locked up with virtually no contact with the outside world, other than some books and old rerun TV shows that he was allowed to watch from a small television which was sometimes rolled in front of the inch thick plexiglass observation window, that was built into his cell door.

The prisoners, even the death row inmates, were allowed to read books from the prison library to pass the time, albeit they were mostly hard to read since there were always pages missing or desecrated.

However, sometimes a good one would make it through the gauntlet.

Oscar would often hear the book cart being wheeled down the corridor, and the rutkis that some of the other inmates were making as they complained about the old and mutilated books and magazines.

When the cart would finally arrive at Oscar's cell, he always kindly asked if there was anything related to the outside world, such as a newspaper that he could read.

The cart librarian was a young and recently married female corrections officer named Marie Kahuta.

She was new to the death row maximum security ward, and in charge of the bi weekly book cart.

Even though she was warned not to supply Oscar with any outside news media, she didn't see the harm in handing over an occasional fictional tabloid.

Especially considering that the staples holding the paper together had been removed.

When available, she would sometimes slip one of the crumpled and outdated fake newspapers through the door slot into Oscar's cell, and reminded him that if he made a mess of it, that it would end his ability to receive them in the future.

Twice a week at around 9 AM, Officer Kahuta passed by with her book cart and Oscar pleasantly returned a book or the neatly folded paper and joked about one of the ridiculous stories that he had previously read in the tabloid.

She would laugh and become distracted as she would retrieve the paper and hand him another one.

As the time went on, she developed a twisted fondness for Oscar, just as Tracy Fernandez, the

teacher that he murdered at the mental institution had done.

What she failed to realize was that Oscar was manipulating her into trusting him, and sooner or later in his diabolical mind, somehow he was going to kill that slut.

It was approximately 9:15 AM, and once again Officer Kahuta arrived with her book cart and she stopped in front of Oscar's cell door.

She opened the auxiliary door slot and Oscar handed her the book that she had left with him a few days prior.

"How was the book?" she questioned.

"Too gorey, even for me!" Oscar chuckled.

She then passed on to Oscar an abused and faded tabloid which she had discovered in an old stack of newspapers in the prison's library, and without noticing that it was crumpled and folded in a manner that the cover was hidden, she passed it through to Oscar and then she continued on her way.

Oscar took the paper and settled down on his bed as he began reading the paper backwards from back to front as he typically did.

It was pretty much the same old thing, with aliens from outer space invading the White house and a wild gorilla that was discovered in the Congo with two heads.

But when he finally turned to the front page, he was in a state of shock when he read the headline;

"WONDER RAMA IS OSCAR'S SPAWN!"

As he went on to read the story, he quickly learned that Rebecca's husband, Charlie was the owner of Maxwell's drug store in Denver, and he was surprised

to find out that after all these years he had actually impregnated Rebecca that night when he raped her, and she had twin daughters, one of which was his and the other was Charlies.

And, it seemed that the apple hadn't fallen far from the tree since daddy's little girl had the same enlarged brain organs as he did!

Oscar was exhilarated with pride that he had actually reproduced, and he believed that his offspring would continue his genetic path and kill all of the sluts in the world.

But in his twisted mind, he believed she was being locked up and abused by Charlie and his family, just as he once was by his parents and step sisters.

Now more than ever, Oscar was determined to get the hell out of that prison cell and hunt down and kill Rebecca, Charlie and Grace, and reclaim his daughter from them, so that they could join forces together and create havoc throughout the world and kill all of the sluts.

Oscar instantly began to devise a devious plan in his corrupted brain, and it was unfolding rapidly as he was preparing to make his move and break out of the escape proof high security prison.

If Oscar were to get out, he would be the first and only prisoner to ever escape the ADMAX prison, and he was confident that by the end of the week, he would become a free man and finish the job he started, only this time with his daughter, Wonder at his side.

They'll hunt down and kill those sluts Rebecca and her daughter Grace, and finish off Charlie once and for all!

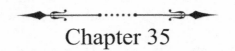

Chapter 35

A week had passed and it was exactly 9 AM.

Officer Kahuta was right on schedule with her book cart, and Oscar could hear the small talk and chatter as she was conversing with the other inmates down the row.

Every few minutes he heard the book cart roll closer, followed by some louder small talk, and then the narrow metal auxiliary door slot would clank open and then slammed closed.

She was getting closer and coming his way.

When Officer Kahuta finally arrived at Oscar's cell, she smiled and had already prepared another tabloid newspaper for him.

When she opened the auxiliary door slot in his cell door, he thanked her for trusting him with the newspapers, and then began pushing the one he was returning back to her through the slot.

However, he carelessly dropped it and fumbled to pick it up, and since the staples had been removed, the paper began falling apart.

He recklessly shuffled it back together and tried to pass it through the slot again, as Officer kahuda impatiently waited.

She was in a hurry, and she carelessly began reaching through the slot to take hold of the loose papers.

Oscar immediately grabbed hold of the young woman's wrist with both of his hands, and began to violently yank her arm back and forth through the slot, over and over again!

He was thrashing her mercilessly against the metal cell door, as if he was trying to pull her through the narrow opening and into his cell!

He managed to pull off her diamond wedding band and he threw it under his bunk during his assault, and she was screaming at the top of her lungs and yelling for help as her head was pounding against Oscar's cell door! Her horrific screams alerted the guards of her onslaught, and two correction officers on duty came rushing over to her aid!

Oscar had clogged his toilet with a hand towel and had been urinating on it all night.

When he saw that one of the correction officers was going to hit the "sleeping gas" button, Oscar released her arm and then he discreetly turned away and removed the urine saturated hand towel from the toilet bowl, and covered his face with it, as he fell down on the floor face down!

However, this was part of his master skeem and he was actually breathing through the urine soaked face cloth, and using it as a makeshift gas mask.

The sleeping gas quickly filled his cell and Oscar pretended to be knocked out and unconscious.

He heard Officer Kahuta cry out that her head was split open and her arm was broken, and that Oscar had taken her wedding ring from her, and tossed it under his bunk.

The three guards quickly put on their masks and were preparing to open Oscar's cell, as Oscar

pretended to be unconscious and waited for his moment.

When they opened his door, all three of the guards entered his cell and the two male guards began kicking and beating Oscar as they believed he was unconscious and incapasitated, while Officer Kahuta feebly searched for her wedding band under the bed.

Oscar's adrenal glands were pumping out quarts of adrenalin into his bloodstream as the two guards viciously attacked him!

Then suddenly he leapt up from his false sleep, and caught them all by surprise!

The guards panicked and struggled to escape, as Oscar instantly and furiously began beating the living hell out of them, and as the fight ensued, Oscar was becoming stronger and stronger!

It was over quite quickly, considering none of the guards were prepared to fight someone with superhuman abilities, and they were all brutally beaten and scattered about, possibly dead or unconscious on the cell floor.

It didn't really matter to Oscar, who only had one thing on his mind, to escape!

Oscar quickly undressed one of the guards and put his uniform on, and then locked the three guards into his cell.

The neighboring inmates heard the tumult and began screaming when they saw that Oscar had escaped from his cell, and they begged Oscar to let them out and take them with him.

He ignored them as he collected a jumble of keys from the guard station and began heading down the corridor to freedom!

As he meanedered his way through the hallways of the ADMAX prison. He waved to the guards as they cheerfully opened gates and doors for him so that he could pass through, until incredibly he walked out the final passageway and was suddenly standing outside in the unsecured prison parking lot, with the sun shining down upon him!

He confidently looked up at the blue sky and deeply drew in the cool fresh morning air through his nostrils, and began to chuckle to himself.

He had done it...

He had escaped from the ADMAX!

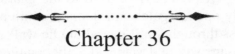

Chapter 36

Oscar didn't waste any time getting away, and he scurried out of the employee parking lot, leaving the ADMAX prison behind him.

When he was sure he was out of view from the prison's security cameras, he began his odd monkey trot down the road to freedom.

However, the prison was situated in an open space area and he found himself on a road in the middle of nowhere.

|He noticed a taxi that was pulled over on the shoulder about a quarter mile down the road, and with no other options and desperate to get away, he quickly headed towards it.

Oscar quickly trotted down the road, opened the cab's back door and hopped into the car.

The driver was a black man in his mid thirties and he looked over his shoulder and coarsely stated;

"Where too, Officer Do Right?"

"Maxwell's drug store, in Denver, and make it quick," Oscar calmly stated.

"That's gonna cost ya, my man," the driver replied.

Oscar removed the correction guard's wallet from his pants pocket and flashed it at the driver.

The driver nodded and put the car in gear and aggressively took off, leaving the massive prison complex behind them.

The taxi was speeding along as there was little traffic that time of the morning, however Oscar did notice several police cars with their lights and sirens blaring, racing towards them and heading towards the prison.

"The word must have gotten out that I escaped," Oscar thought.

It took about 60 minutes for the taxi to finally arrive at the drugstore, and when the cab stopped the fare was $295 dollars.

Oscar directed the driver to pull into the parking lot behind the drug store and when the car stopped, the driver was suspicious and feared that Oscar might make a run for it and stiff him on his hefty cab fare.

The driver immediately jumped out of his car carrying a long wooden billy club and opened Oscar's door, blocking his possible escape, and he demanded his money.

Oscar reached for the wallet, and when he opened it, he realized that it contained only $35 dollars!

He matter of factly smiled and then sadly revealed his lack of funds to the taxi driver.

The driver became extremely agitated and grabbed hold of Oscar and dragged him out of his cab and proceeded to beat him with his wooden club!

In a matter of seconds, Oscar easily overpowered the man and took hold of his billy club!

He effortlessly threw the cab driver into the backseat of the taxi and proceeded to strangle the man with one hand, as he brutally clubbed the man's face and shattered his skull with his other hand!

When he was done killing the driver, he pointed his nose up into the air and filled his nostrils with the

scent of death and then passionately kissed the man's obliterated face as he pushed himself off of him.

He cautiously peeked out of the cab, looking to see if anyone had witnessed the murder, but it seemed that there was no one around and he was in the clear.

As Oscar left the taxi, he quietly closed its door and noticed a sign in a secluded part of the parking lot which read "EMPLOYEE PARKING," and so he swaggered over and began peering into the vehicles.

He instantly noticed that in a certain pickup truck that was parked there, there were a pair of identical Castle Rock high school team windbreakers tossed recklessly on the back seat.

"This has to be that dirtbag Charlie's truck," Oscar thought, and he opened the tailgate and crawled under the bed cover and laid in wait for Charlie to bring him home to his blood daughter.

Meanwhile back at the ADMAX, the prison was in chaos as the alarms were blaring and lights were flashing!

Scores of state police vehicles filled the prison's parking lot, and the search was on.

They were all desperately looking for Oscar.

No one ever expected that he or any other prisoner could ever pull off that sort of escape.

Somewhere along the way, Oscar had discovered that urine and the ammonia contained in it, was used during WWI as a makeshift gas mask, and it was his ace in the hole when the time was right.

He manipulated the correction officer into lowering her guard with him, and he seized the opportunity and initiated his plan.

Police were swarming the entire area and there was an all points bulletin out for Oscar.

The FBI, and other local authorities were all on the lookout for the nations most violent psychopathic killer to ever to have been locked up at the high security prison, and the whole state of Colorado was under lockdown.

Charlie couldn't believe his ears when he heard the bulletin on the radio that Oscar Demento had escaped the Florence ADMAX, and was on the run.

He feared that Oscar might track them down and could possibly show up at their farm.

It was about 6 PM and Charlie, being on edge, decided to close up his drug store early.

But before he left, he took two large hypodermic syringes and a full vial of some sort of mysterious drug, and the 357 magnum revolver that he kept behind the counter, and spun the cylinder verifying that it was fully loaded and ready to shoot.

He placed the items in his briefcase and slid the gun awkwardly into his front pants pocket and nervously left the store.

As he approached his truck he noticed the abandoned taxi cab, and that the driver was nowhere to be found.

He thought it was odd, but he had other things on his mind and it wasn't uncommon for people to leave their cars in his parking lot overnight.

As he unlocked his truck he had an imminent gut feeling that something was not right, and so he withdrew his gun from his front pocket and aggressively opened the truck's door, and checked the back seat area to see if anyone was hiding back there!

He was relieved to see that the compartment was empty and chuckled to himself that he was being overly paranoid, and that there was no possible way Oscar could have ever tracked them down while being on the run from the police.

|He jumped into his truck, started the engine and quickly darted out of the parking lot, unknowingly carrying the deranged psychopathic killer back to his farm and family.

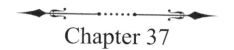

Chapter 37

It was approximately 6:35 PM when Charlie barreled into his crushed stone driveway.

The sun had set and it was just beginning to get dark.

He rushed out of the truck and barged through the porch door and charged into the house.

"Rebecca! Rebecca! Where are you?" Charlie shouted.

Rebecca came rushing out of the kitchen with her apron on and wearing oven mitts.

"I'm baking a cake! What's going on Charlie!?" she anxiously replied.

"There is terrible news, Rebecca. Oscar escaped from the prison and he is on the loose! They have been looking for him all day with no luck!" Charlie exclaimed.

"He doesn't know where we live, Charlie. He'll never find us out here in the middle of nowhere! Besides, he is probably hiding out somewhere in the mountains near the prison, and he has no money or means to get around," Rebecca stated.

Suddenly there was a loud knock at the back door.

Charlie nervously fumbled to remove his gun from his trousers and then anxiously peeked out through a side window to see who was there.

He noticed a man wearing some sort of police uniform and he was partially hidden from view and seemed anxious.

Believing it to be a police officer, Charlie rushed over to the back door;

"Who is it?!"

"Uh Mr. Rama, I'm... I'm uh, Officer Clark with the Castle rock Police department. As you are probably aware by now, Oscar Demento broke out of the ADMAX in Florence, and considering that you and your family have some history with that psychopathic freek, the chief thought it best that I keep an eye on things over here. Please open the door!" the officer ordered.

Charlie paused, then reluctantly opened the door, just as the police had turned away and was looking out towards the barn as if he was suddenly distracted by some unusual movement.

The officer then turned back and instantly glanced down at Charlie's handgun, and the way he was awkwardly holding it.

"Is that weapon loaded, Sir?" the police officer questioned.

Charlie nodded "yes" that it was.

"Maybe I better hold on to that gun for you son, since you don't look like you have ever used a gun before," suggested the police officer.

Charlie reluctantly handed over the gun, and the officer took it and tucked it behind his belt.

"You won't have to worry, that lunatic is probably hiding out in some dumpster outside the prison. Just for your peace of mind though, I'll be camped out here all night," stated the police officer.

The officer then marched over to his car and backed it next to the barn, where it was out of sight from the road and house, and he turned off the lights.

It was quite dark out, and so he reclined in his seat and covered his face with his policemans hat to block out the light coming from the spotlight over the barn door, and he decided to take a nap.

Charlie felt a bit more at ease knowing that a police officer was outside his home, as he helped Rebecca mix the frosting for the cake she had baked, when it suddenly dawned on him that the twins were not there.

"Rebecca! Where are the girls!" Charlie exclaimed.

"They were at field hockey practice at school. One of the parents is taking some of the girls out for supper and then they are going to drop them off at home," Rebecca replied.

"I'm going to go outside to warn the cop that the girls will be coming home from school shortly," Charlie stated.

Charlie then pushed the back door open and walked toward the police cruiser.

He stepped into a greasy puddle on the ground near the driver's side door of the police cruiser, and noticed the officer was already sleeping on the job with his seat partially reclined, and his face covered by his large policemans hat.

Charlie knocked on the window several times and noticed that the officer was seemingly sound asleep and wouldn't wake up.

"Hey!! Officer Clark!! Wake up, my kids are going to be home shortly and I don't want you shooting at them!" Charlie joked.

But there was dead silence and no movement from the officer.

Charlie sensed something was wrong, and took hold of the door handle and cautiously opened the cruiser's door.

The compartment light turned on and he instantly became sickened when he saw that the officer was reclined in his seat and his uniform was soaked with the same dark liquid he had stepped into outside his car, blood!!

Charlie carefully took hold of the wide brim of the officer's policemans hat which was covering his face, and as he lifted it, he could see the horrific gaze of death on the officer's face!

Instantly his neck had just given way and his grotesque decapitated head rolled off the top of his neck and dropped down into his lap!

Charlie began screaming as he realized that there was only one person who could have done this!

Oscar the deranged psychopath had found them!

Frantically, Charlie searched for the handset of the police radio but it was recklessly torn from the radio and nowhere to be found!

Suddenly Charlie heard a scream coming from his house!

Desperately he searched for the policeman's gun holster, but his gun was gone.

However his 357 magnum was just lying there under the decapitated officer's head, on his blood soaked lap.

Rebecca screamed again and Charlie awkwardly rolled the officers head to the floor, and he took his

gun and scrambled from the police cruiser, and was rushing back to the house to save Rebecca!

When he stormed back into the house, he found Oscar heavily splattered with blood and dressed as a corrections officer, clutching Rebecca from behind by her long blonde hair, while holding a bloody sickle blade knife tightly hooked around her neck!

"I hope you don't mind me borrowing this tool from your barn, I severed that cop's head off with just one whack! I don't know why I was wasting my time with that butcher's cleaver all those years. I like this sickle knife much better!" Oscar snickered.

Rebecca was petrified as Oscar began sniffing and licking her neck as he kept his gaze on Charlie.

"Let her go, Oscar! Don't you have even a drop of righteousness in your soul?" Charlie desperately pleaded and he raised his gun and pointed it at Oscar's face.

"The only righteous thing I have is my daughter," Oscar shouted and he threw Rebecca at Charlie.

The gun went off when they collided and when the smoke cleared, Oscar was lying motionless on the floor, with one hand over the side of his belly, and the other still holding the sickle knife.

"Shoot him again, Charlie!!" Rebecca shouted.

Charlie was dazed and petrified.

He had never shot anyone before and that gun suddenly weighed 1000 lbs.

Charlie froze as Oscar began to move and he realized he was only grazed by Charlie's bullet!

"Hurry up!! Shoot him again Charlie!!" Rebecca screamed and Charlie squinted as he once again pulled the trigger, however there was no loud bang,

and only a click from the gun's hammer hitting the empty chamber.

Oscar began to chuckle as he reached into his shirt pocket and revealed the bullets that he had previously removed from the gun.

"That cop shouldn't have been sleeping on the job! I guess I forgot about the bullet in the chamber when I emptied the gun," Oscar heinously laughed as he crept back onto his feet, and devilishly inhaled their terrified stench back through his nostrils.

Oscar then reached out and motioned for Charlie to hand over the empty gun, as he faciously began swinging his sickle blade at him.

Charlie threw the gun on the floor and Rebecca stood there frozen with fear as Oscar picked up the gun and then placed one bullet back into the revolver.

He spun the cylinder and pointed the gun at Charlie's head and pulled the trigger as Charlie squinted and tried to duck away!

Nothing happened, and Oscar let out a loud boisterous laugh.

"Okay, now it's my slutty girlfriend's turn," and Oscar spun the gun's cylinder once again and aimed the gun directly at Rebecca's head! Charlie charged at Oscar and tried to take hold of the gun but Oscar was too strong and knocked him to the floor with a single powerful blow to the head from the butt of the pistol.

Charlie was knocked unconscious, and was incapasitated!

"Now look at what you made me do. I was just starting to have some fun!" complained Oscar and he aimed the gun at Charlie's head and pulled the trigger.

But once again, nothing happened.

Oscar then began repeatedly squeezing the trigger, anticipating that at some point the cartridge would align and he would put a bullet into Charlie's skull.

Rebecca, fearing for Charlie's life, lunged at Oscar and pushed his arm away just as the gun had fired what would have been a fatal shot into Charlie's head!

He laughed and grabbed Rebecca once again by her long blond hair and effortlessly dragged her down into the basement.

She struggled with all her might but it was no use, Oscar was just too strong.

He used a piece of cord and tied her arms up to a steel water pipe that was attached to the basement ceiling, and as she hung there she hopelessly begged and pleaded for their lives as he pulled her legs apart and tied each one to the opposing steel columns which ran down the length of the basement.

Oscar then returned upstairs and dragged Charlie's unconscious body clumsily down the steps to the basement, and was preparing to slice his head off with the sickle knife, when Rebecca started screaming hysterically for him to stop!!

Oscar momentarily froze as he caught a whiff of her feminine scent and he lifted his nose up in the air and inhaled her aroma, and it distracted him.

He began to get aroused and he dropped Charlie's limp body and moved up behind Rebecca.

He began to sniff and investigate her body as she hung there helplessly, and he began erotically licking her sweaty skin with his long slithering tongue.

He hung his sickle knife around her neck, just as someone would hang a hat on a coat hook, and then he began to reach around her and embraced her tightly as he groped her breasts and pulled himself into her body.

"Oooh yes, now I remember you. What kind of a girl has sex with a total stranger on the first date? You my dear are a slut! And I know how to deal with a slut!!" Oscar shouted at the top of his lungs.

He was charged and preparing to sexually violate her again as he reached under her dress and tore off her underwear!

He then dropped to his knees and lifted the back of her dress over his head, and slowly began caressing his filthy bloodstained fingers up her naked legs and then up between her inner thighs as she helplessly hung there and struggled to break free of her bindings.

He then pressed his face into the back of her leg and licked her perspiring skin as his grotesque fingers engulfed her thigh and continued to slyther upward between her legs.

He was about to feel her, and she felt his fingers approaching and she began to struggle furiously, desperately trying to shake his hands off of her!

However, the ropes were too tight and her resistance only enticed Oscar even more.

Just as Oscar was about to penetrate her with his fingers, there was suddenly a loud knock at the front door.

Oscar instantly stopped and became frustrated.

"Why can't I ever have any "Me" time!!!" he hysterically ranted.

He reluctantly stopped and took hold of the sickle knife from Rebecca's neck and raced up the stairs, traveling in his monkey trot, and peeked through the basement doorway to see who was at the front door.

At first he thought it might be his daughter, Wonder coming home.

But then he heard that it was a man, nervously pounding on the door.

"Charlie! Rebecca! Let me in! Oscar is on the loose and I came over to warn you!" shouted Rebecca's father.

Oscar, who was aching to get back to Rebecca, charged towards the door, ripped it open and took hold of Mr. Kannon, and without any thought or hesitation drove the sickle blade deeply into his heart, and laughed as he lifted him up with his blade and drew him closer.

Rebecca's father was stunned and caught off guard as Oscar dragged him into the house and threw him on top of the kitchen table and swiftly amputated his head with another vicious blow from his sickle knife!

Rebecca hung there, desperately trying to untie herself when she heard something thumping down the basement stairs like a bowling ball, and then Oscars heavy steps were following behind it, back down to the basement.

To her horror when she glanced over, she saw that it was her fathers severed head staring back at her from the base of the staircase and that Oscar had rolled it down the stairs after killing him!

Rebecca began to shriek and scream at the top of her lungs and Oscar quickly stripped and became naked, and began to aggressively fondle himself.

He savored his perverted thoughts of picking up where he had left off and approached her from behind, and began groping his bloody hand all over Rebecca's breasts as he molested her down below with his other hand, and he pulled himself tightly into her quivering body.

"Time to breed, again, Slut-ski!" Oscar whispered into her ear and he delicately began lifting up the back of her dress as he inhaled her scent, and he was aligning himself to violate her again.

Then suddenly there was a loud "thud" which came from the other side of the basement!

It sounded as if the basement hatchway door had dropped closed, and Oscar quickly looked over to Charlie and saw that he was gone!

Charlie had suddenly revived, and knew he was no match for Oscar and he needed to get help!

"Son of a Bitch!!! Can't a deranged psychopath get any action around here!!" Oscar screamed.

Oscar became wild with rage and ran after Charlie, bursting through the wooden hatchway doors, and he ran off into the darkness sniffing the air and searching for Charlie's scent.

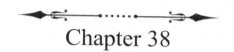

Chapter 38

The twins were singing songs and carrying on in the back of the minivan, as they were on their way home from field hockey practice and a late supper with a few of their High school teammates.

It was dark and they were getting home later than they expected.

Their ride dropped them off at the end of their driveway, and they both thanked the parents and said their goodbyes, and then they raced each other to their front porch door.

It was eerily quiet in their yard and they noticed their fathers truck in the driveway with its bed cover ripped and torn apart, and their grandfather's car was oddly parked there too, considering that he rarely comes over, and the lights were all out and it seemed that no one was home.

"Mom! Dad! GrandPa!" Grace shouted.

But there was no response, just dead silence.

When they cautiously entered the kitchen they found a bloody mess, and it appeared that a fight had ensued.

As they investigated the crime scene, they were horrified to find the body of their estranged grandfather, who was hunched over on the floor with his upper body stuffed inside the open oven!

Grace placed her hand softly on his back and gently began pulling him out when Wonder took hold of her hand, and stopped her just in time.

A moment before she would reveal that his body was disfigured, and his head was totally chopped off!

Immediately the twins noticed that the basement door was open and they heard their mom moaning and calling for help once she heard that the twins had come home.

They immediately charged down the stairs, and Grace rushed to her mother and quickly began uniting her tightly bound hands and legs.

Rebecca instantly collapsed, as she was mentally exhausted and barely conscious.

Wonder saw that the basement hatchway was obliterated and raced out through it, searching for her father and the intruder.

"Grace, Grace! Call the police! Oscar is going to kill us!" Rebecca moaned.

Grace immediately charged up the basement steps and when she turned the corner into the kitchen she was mortified to find Oscar naked and standing there with his sickle blade dripping with blood!

She was paralyzed with fear as Oscar raised the crescent blade and ambled toward her with his hideous monkey trot.

He raised his diabolical blade, and drew his arm back to deliver a lethal decapitation strike!

Grace screamed a deathly shriek and crossed her hands in front of her face and closed her eyes, as Oscar mercilessly advanced toward her!

The front door suddenly burst open and Wonder came charging into the house!

She dove through the air and hit Oscar so hard he crashed into the kitchen table, smashing it to pieces!

"Get out of here, Grace!!" Wonder shouted.

Grace managed to run upstairs to her room and she picked up the phone but she instantly realized that the phone was dead and out of order!

Oscar slowly got up, stretched his jaw and hideously smiled at Wonder.

"So you are supposed to be my spawn, daughter. What the hell is wrong with you? Let's join together and slaughter these scumbags that molested and abused you," Oscar maniacally babbled.

Wonder was charged and her own overactive adrenal glands were on fire!

"You may be my father, but you're certainly not my Dad!" Wonder shouted.

She picked up a broken table leg and Oscar lunged at her, and he began swinging his sickle blade furiously in an attempt to kill her.

She was amazing as she continued to block Oscar's flailing blade with some form of martial arts maneuvers and the wooden table leg that she clutched in her hands, and the two became entangled in a vicious fight!

She knew that her father was stronger than her despite her super strength, and she couldn't keep up the fight much longer, and finally her wooden table leg gave out and broke in two!

She threw the two pieces at him and then lifted the kitchen table from the floor, and plowed it into him.

He was knocked to the ground, but it gave her a moment to get away from him, and she ran out of the farm house!

Grace then came rushing down the stairs and Oscar reached over and grabbed her by her leg as she tried to run past him!

He easily pulled her down and then dragged her closer, as she was kicking and screaming for help!

He stood up and wrapped his hand around her throat and threw her up against the kitchen wall, pinning her there approximately 3 feet above the floor!

She screamed and struggled to get away from him, but he was too strong and he began to strangle her with his bare hand as she kicked at him and flailed against the wall!!

Charlie returned to the basement and crept up the staircase, holding the two hypodermic syringes that he had left in his briefcase in his truck.

They were both fully loaded with the drug Metoprolol which he had taken from his pharmacy.

He courageously dove on top of Oscar as he was strangling Grace, and injected one of the powerful doses of the drug into Oscar's neck!

Oscar instantly released his hold on Grace and she fell to the floor, and he then turned to Charlie!

Oscar lunged at him with his sickle knife when he suddenly felt the effects of the drug, and that his strength was quickly diminishing!

Oscar began stumbling on his feet as Charlie grabbed hold of a chair and broke it over Oscar's head, and then he desperately rushed over to tend to Grace who was totally unconscious, but still barely alive.

Oscar fell to the floor and was dazed by the strike, and although he was in a weakened state, he was still extremely dangerous.

Oscar regained his senses and took hold of the broken chair and managed to get himself up off the floor, and then came up behind Charlie as he was trying to revive Grace.

He clenched his teeth and cocked his arm as he began to swing the sickle blade, aiming directly at Charlie's neck!

Grace's eyes barely began to open when she noticed Oscar approaching from behind her father with his bloody blade cocked and ready to strike him, and she screamed!

Charlie turned and attempted to jump away as Oscar swung!

Oscar missed his mark and stuck the hooked blade into the side of Charlie's torso!

Charlie tripped and instantly fell over onto the floor as Oscar pried out the blade and quickly drew his arm back once again for a decapitating strike!

Suddenly, Wonder came charging back into the house, this time armed with her field hockey stick!

She began swinging it furiously and was brutally bludgeoning Oscar in his weakened state with her hefty wooden stick!

Rebecca managed to climb up from the basement and immediately tended to Charlie, who was holding his hand over his gaping wound to keep the blood from pouring out, and with his other hand, trying to tend to Grace.

Wonder continued her vicious assault on Oscar, as now she was the stronger of the two.

The drug Charlie had injected was working, and had instantly neutralized Oscar's powers, but not for long.

With whatever strength he had left, Oscar frantically managed to escape Wonder's onslaught by covering his head and scrambling out of the house!

Wonder then ceased her assault and helped Rebecca tend to Charlie and Grace.

Oscar was hurting and desperate to get away, when he noticed a light hanging over a basketball hoop above the barn door.

He felt that if he could "lay low" until the drug wore off, he could then return and finish them all off!

He staggered into the barn still clutching onto his sickle blade, and he carefully maneuvered around the long spears of the old farm tractors front hay loader which were pointing up towards the hayloft.

He instantly noticed a ladder extending up to the hayloft, and thought it would be a good place to hide until the Metoprolol was out of his system.

He began climbing up the dilapidated ladder, which was mounted to the wall, and it extended up through an open trap door to the hay loft.

This was the first time in his life that Oscar had ever used a ladder, and he climbed awkwardly upward as he clung to the handle of his horrific blade with one hand, and the rungs of the ladder with the other.

As he approached the top of the ladder, he could hear the faint sound of a litter of stray kittens meowing up there.

"Although I despise cats, what harm could a bunch of kittens do? Maybe I could slit their throats and gut

them, as I wait for the drug to wear off, " he chuckled to himself.

Oscar finally reached the top of the ladder and grabbed hold of the final rung with his free hand.

His head was just rising up through the opening of the trap door into the hayloft, when a ferocious ginger striped mom cat lashed out and attacked his face as he popped up through the hole into the loft!

She viciously hissed and hauntingly screamed as she shredded his face with her razor sharp claws, as she was fiercely protecting her kittens!

Oscar was deathly afraid of her and caught off guard!

He instantly lurched backward and lost his grip, falling backwards off of the ladder, and his body landed squarely on top of the long, sharp protruding spikes of the tractor's hay loader!

He was harpooned and dangling there while his blood dripped out of his contorted body, hideously skewered by the deadly row of the sharp pointed hay spikes!

Despite his deadly impalement, he was still alive and was struggling to free himself as he began coughing up blood.

Wonder had just appeared and stopped in the barn doorway, when she saw that Oscar was impaled on the long metal spears of the tractor's loader.

When Oscar noticed his daughter standing there, he strained and spoke to her;

"Oscarette Demento is your real name. One day that switch will flick inside your head and then you'll be just like me, a deranged psychopath!" Oscar moaned.

Wonder lifted her nose to the air and inhaled his scent and a crazed look came over her.

She entered the barn and picked up the bloody sickle knife he had dropped when he fell from the ladder.

The massive amount of adrenalin racing through her body seemed to change her, and she approached her skewered and dying father.

She stood beside him and leaned over to her father and tenderly ran her fingers through his deranged and greasy long red hair, and then seductively licked the blood from the side of his face and whispered;

"I'm so sorry Father, but I'm not Oscarette Dimento. I'm Wonder Rama, and that switch went off inside my head a long time ago, I just managed to hide it better than you!"

Oscar's face lit up and he was giddy and overcome with joy as he instantly realized that his daughter was a deranged psychopath just like himself, and she had been concealing it from everyone, laying in wait until she was ready to expose herself.

Oscar attempted to maniacally laugh as he coughed up more blood and began choking.

He took great pleasure knowing that his seed was alive and within her, and she was just like him!

"Let's go kill Charlie and those Sluts!" Oscar strained.

And then he noticed in her hand, that she was gripping tightly onto the bloody sickle knife!

Oscar laughed and began hideously barking out as if he were an excited ape, as he now knew that she was a crazed psychopath just like him.

She smiled and then clenched his long red hair, and then she stretched his head upward and back, fully exposing his throat, as she drew back the sickle blade that was in her other hand!

With a glowing smile on her face and a jovial decisive swing, she completely decapitated her father's head!

As the blood splattered and gushed out everywhere, she raised his head and kissed his morbid face, and then she calmly turned and left the barn, tossing her fathers head up at the old basketball hoop which hung over the barn door.

Wonder was emboldened now, and rather than continue to suppress her gruesome psychopathic appetite, she stalked back to the house where her parents and sister were huddled on the kitchen floor, unaware of Oscar's death and unsure if he would return to finish them off, as they waited for the police and ambulances to arrive.

Her eyes were crazed and her mind was deranged as she stood there on the porch, and looked in through the doorway of her home as her mother tended to Charlie's wounds, and Grace was massaging her throat and still trying to catch her breath.

Wonder's body was still supercharged with adrenalin, and then a powerful urge came over her.

And Wonder lifted her nose up and deeply inhaled the vial fragrance of blood and death in the air.

Something innate and diabolical had taken a strong hold of her.

She had tasted blood and the decapitating death of her father was deeply gratifying to her.

She maniacally laughed and felt an uncontrollable craving to sadistically slaughter and cause gruesome bodily harm, and it was overwhelming her!

But that was her family in there, and as much as she loved them, there was an uncontrollable and insatiable urge to savagely slaughter them all.

There were demonic voices echoing in her head that began to scream and shout at her!

"Kill them all, before they kill you, Wonder!"

"Those creatures in there are not your family anymore!

They are actually a race of parasitic brain-sucking space aliens, from the planet Bizarro! They already killed your parents and sister, by sucking their brains out. Once they get a hold of you, they'll fire a gruesome, slimy, spiked feeding tube out of their mouths, and it will drill deeply into your skull! Then they'll homogenize your brain, so they can completely suck it out for supper!

You need to get in there and kill those bastards, before they get you too!!" the sinister voices shrieked.

Wonder struggled because in some remote part of her brain she knew it was far fetched and wrong.

She fought the impulse to kill her family, she loved them dearly, but she struggled in her demented mind that they were vicious alien preditors from outer space, and she must slaughter them all, and save the world!

And so she crouched down and subtly began vocalizing as if she were a wild chimp, just as her father had always done.

And Wonder's ape chatter became louder and louder, as her psychosis had taken its hold over her, as she approached the front door!

Her family noticed her out on the porch looking in through the doorway, and they became concerned when they saw her behaving oddly and staring at them in a maniacal way, and so they joined hands and prayed for her.

And then Wonder drew back her bloody sickle knife, and she swiftly bolted into the house, whooping and galloping in like a raging chimp, and she slammed the door shut behind her!

Short and Sharp...

Made in United States
North Haven, CT
17 June 2023

37902400R00136